D1525461

Birds On A Wire Media
3201 Browns Mill Road Ste 6 #211
Johnson City, TN 37604
www.birdsonawiremedia.com

For information for speaking events or interviews with the author go to: georgiacurtisling.com

Dedicated to the heavyhearted little boy who placed an ornament of hope on his tree and experienced a Christmas miracle that blessed his life forever.

Contents

the Ornament of Hope

Sometimes in loss...
you discover *love.*

georgia curtis ling

BIRDS ON A WIRE MEDIA

THE ORNAMENT OF HOPE
BY
Georgia Curtis Ling

*Dedicated to the heavyhearted little boy who placed
an ornament of hope on his tree and experienced
a Christmas miracle that blessed his life forever.*

Chapter One

W *hat have I done?*

The question had played on an endless loop in Shauna's head for the past six hours. She turned on her signal to exit off the highway for the final five-mile drive home and swore the clicking from the blinker chirped like a Mockingbird, asking again in rhythm, *What have I done? What have I done?*

Hours before, when she'd packed her Jeep and the GPS pointed her north, there was only an outline of the mountain range as the sun set. The darkness slowly crept in to conceal the mountains as she left her old life and the city lights of Atlanta in her rear-view mirror and headed over the pass through the Chattahoochee and Cherokee National Forest, once inhabited long ago by the Cherokee and Creek Indians. She recalled the Native American and Appalachian folklore stories she'd heard around late-night campfires of their ghosts that still roamed the dense forest around mysterious ruins after midnight. By day, you could hike past these shapeshifters camouflaged as harmless little squirrels, but at night they stalk the mountains, guarding their forest, walking amongst the camps of hikers who settle in under the canopy of trees for their night of recovery.

Those stories floated in her brain, which made for a spooky drive. She hoped they were only tall tales and she wouldn't catch a glimpse of any ghosts lurking on the side of the road during her solitary drive. However, with the bad fortune that had kept knocking on Shauna Murphy's door recently, her Irish luck seemed to be running low, so chances were pretty good this would be the night for a sighting. She kept her eyes peeled as she drove along the highway.

Griping the steering wheel with one hand, she took a swig from her water bottle. Suddenly, the emergency weather alert on her cell phone blared, causing her to throw the water bottle across the front seat. That got her attention. She fumbled for the phone for the mute button, and read the black-ice warning. Just as her heart calmed, the phone rang and it almost joined her water bottle somewhere on the passenger seat. Somehow, she held on to the phone. This call was a welcome visitor.

"Hi, Mom!"

"Hi, hon, just checking in to see how the trip is going. I was a little worried when I saw the weather forecast. Are the roads slick?" She wasn't just a little worried, Colleen always worried. A lot.

Shauna thought it was nice to have a little distraction from the thoughts of ghosts.

"Everything is good so far, the traffic is light, but just before you called the weather alert came over the phone and scared me half to death." She maneuvered around a semi slowly climbing the hill.

"Just wanted to let you know the guest cottage is ready. I turned up the heat to take the chill off the air. We had a big Black Friday sale at the shop today. I'm exhausted, so I'm heading to bed early. How are you feeling?"

Shauna heard genuine concern in her mom's voice but, she wasn't ready to pour her heart out over the phone – again.

"I'm good, Mom. I'll fill you in when I get home." The signal started breaking up and saved her. "The signal is br… Get a g… night's sleep. I l… you." The signal dropped.

Just as warned, snow lightly dusted the road and she was on the lookout for black ice and the whitetail deer that fly across the road. Well, not literally, she thought, they're not Santa's flying reindeers, but she had witnessed them gracefully jump over and clear a car without missing a stride and vanish into the wilderness. Shauna grinned when she saw the yellow Deer Crossing caution signs posted on the side of the road. She remembered the story that went viral of the woman who, after three accidents involving deer, called authorities and wanted the signs removed. She was under the impression they were path-finding signs for deer to safely cross, and she wanted them moved to lower-traffic areas. She couldn't understand why they were encouraging deer to cross the interstate. A giggle erupted as Shauna pictured a deer standing on his hindlegs, putting on reading glasses, and checking out the sign. She felt for the lady who became known as "Debbie the Deer Lady." She knew she shouldn't laugh at the expense of others, but it was funny. It felt good to laugh, even if she was laughing by herself. It seemed as if she hadn't laughed once in a blue moon. Jokes aside, she had to be careful. Unfortunately, not all whitetail deer can high-jump a SUV, and she didn't want to leave a helpless victim in her path.

She turned that phase over in her mind – a helpless victim. She was a victim, that was the cold hard truth, she wouldn't dispute that, but she wasn't helpless. Wounded – yes, helpless – no.

She hadn't made the trip home for a long time, but one thing hadn't changed – the mountains. Her hometown of Spring Valley, Tennessee, nestled in the shadow of the Appalachian Mountains, enveloped her like a comforting, cozy quilt. This place always had a soothing effect on Shauna, and she desperately needed to be wrapped in comfort, to calm and heal her hurt.

She knew her history well. Her pioneer ancestors blazed the trails over the mountain range and were attracted to the beauty of the area, it being filled with fresh springs, abundant wild-life, hunting, and rich soil that they needed to survive. They established their settlement beside the spring-water source. The springs continued to draw people to the town as Spring Valley flour-ished. The springs became a life-source.

It was almost midnight when the last mile of the journey welcomed her to downtown Spring Valley, dressed in greens and garlands. A massive fir tree in the center square was adorned with soft twinkling lights. Old-fashioned lanterns, tucked in red-bowed wreaths spread a soft warm glow on Main Street. This was where as a child she had held her daddy's hand, watching the trains pass by; as a teen walked to work and cashed her first paycheck; as a young woman shared her first kiss at the New Year's Eve celebration street dance. Atlanta drew her away to the big city with a dream job that turned into a nightmare. This small historic town beckoned her home, for what, she didn't know. Shauna just worried if this was the right time to return.

This little town was big on celebrating their Appalachian heritage all year long, especially at Christmas. The last thing Shauna wanted to think about was Christmas. If she'd had a wish list, all she wanted was her job back. Her boyfriend back. Her life back. *What she thinking?* She could have delayed coming home until after Christmas. Her parents would have understood.

Right on cue, just like a Hallmark movie, the

snow flurries floated in the air, dusting this whimsical little town. She felt as if she was driving her Jeep in a humongous festive snow globe. But if it were her snow globe she would be knocking over the snowman, snatching the bell out of Santa's white glove, and making a run for it, Grinchly laughing all the way. She was in no mood for the holidays.

It was one of the reasons she'd moved to Atlanta in the first place. Shauna had wanted to escape her 24/7 Christmas life. She'd felt trapped in a never-ending Christmas snow globe. It was quite fun as a toddler living in the fantasy world of your mother's business, but being part of The Olde Town Christmas shop grew tiring year-after-year; being teased and enduring the "Miss Christmas" nickname, not just during the season, but for 365 days! By the time she left for college that was 6,935 days – but who's counting? she thought. Not to mention spending every waking hour after Halloween preparing for the day after Thanksgiving and the kickoff of the annual Appalachian Christmas Heritage Festival, a month-long celebration of the season. She had managed to miss the kickoff this year, but she knew all too well what was in store for this little town. Her head ached just thinking about it. She needed to sleep. She was looking forward to falling into bed, pulling the quilt up over her head and dreaming her worries away.

The guest cottage was tucked in the back

corner of her parents' property. The solitude was just what she needed. It was after midnight. While everyone was fast asleep, all snuggled in their beds, she could slip in to the guest house, unannounced. The corner of her lips lifted, almost creating a smile, when she remembered she wouldn't even have to unpack a thing tonight because she knew her mom would have the snowmen holiday pajamas laid out on the bed, awaiting her twenty-seven-year-old daughter. It was a family holiday tradition.

What she really needed was a place to hide from the holiday hoopla. When she left Atlanta, if she'd had the tiniest bit of a Christmas spirit hidden somewhere deep in her soul, she had definitely lost it somewhere over the mountain pass. *What was she thinking?*

As she pulled into the driveway, all lit up like a runway with sparkling Christmas lights, she was thinking maybe she had made a mistake.

#

Shauna awoke to the loud honking sound of wild Canadian geese that made their winter home on the pond behind the cottage. The local goose whisperer lady, who felt it necessary to disobey the DO NOT FEED THE GEESE AND DUCKS sign, started her morning routine tossing little nuggets of chicken feed to the fat geese and ducks that waddled around her for their breakfast, excitingly honking their gratitude. Shauna pulled a pillow over her head to stifle the sound when another alarm clock of the fowl kind chimed in with the clucking of her mother's chickens singing their "egg song" announcing to their little hen friends that their morning egg-laying chore was complete. Then all the ladies chimed in with a chorus of celebratory cackling and clucking. Shauna thought they must be celebrating really loud since most chickens don't lay eggs in the winter. Her mom's chickens were a hardy and proud bunch. She felt as if she'd awoken in a duck, duck, chicken, goose sanctuary.

She had secretly hoped she would fall into a Rip Van Winkle sound sleep and not wake up until New Year's Day, but thanks to her noisy neighbors, Shauna gave up on that dream. Her late-night snack had worn off and she needed her morning ritual of coffee and hopefully a breakfast pastry from her favorite coffee house waiting for her in her parents' kitchen. She crossed her fingers for a lemon poppyseed muffin or, better yet, maybe a slice of the butter pound cake.

Her room was chilly when she reluctantly threw the covers back, grabbed a robe, rummaged through her luggage for her toiletry bag for a tooth brush and made her way to the bathroom. The mirror greeted her with the reality that her mother's selection of bright-red-and-white snowmen pajamas clashed with her red hair. Her mom knew the old adage that redheads should never wear red, but she was always trying to be her fashion consultant. Shauna shook her head hoping her mother didn't have matching pajamas for the whole family for a group picture. It's not that she didn't like her red hair, she loved it! She loved standing out from the crowd. She just liked wearing flattering colors, not clashing colors. Besides, she thought, who in their right mind would complain about being compared to Nicole Kidman? She wasn't her doppelgänger, but with her sapphire-blue eyes, natural rusty-red hair and creamy complexation lightly dusted with freckles, she came pretty close. It showed when she met a stranger and they gave a second look, just making sure they weren't missing out on a selfie with a celebrity. Shauna puffed a big sigh. Nicole had Keith and she had nobody.

Chapter Two

The pathway to the house sparkled like tiny diamonds, compliments of the early-morning frost. It even gave a nice sheen to the dormant rose bushes that lined the walkway from Rose Cottage to the main house. Hence the name, Rose Cottage. Her gran had lived in the cottage for a few years after her grandfather had passed away. She was the real gardener of the family. New life was announced every spring as the yard burst with color. The fragrant rainbow of romantic roses that wandered beside the path was a testament to the long hours Gran had spent tending the earth. The pruned bushes drew her back to an image of her gran as she clipped back the roses for winter, saying, "The good Lord knew what he was doing in the garden. Every spring is a miracle. The roses need to rest over the winter to build their strength for beautiful spring blooms." Shauna felt as if Gran was whispering in her ear. *Shauna, rest! The good Lord knows what he's doing. Your spring is coming. Don't lose hope, wait for your miracle.* Missing her Gran, her heart felt a twinge of sorrow followed by the soothing thought that Gran was still whispering prayers on her behalf.

Shauna picked up her pace, she regretted

her choice of a robe instead of a coat, and sprinted to the back door. Fortunately, she didn't have to remember a key. Her daddy had upgraded all the locks to a keypad and of course her mother insisted on the code: 1225.

She was greeted with the comforting aroma of coffee and instantly felt a much-needed brain boost.

"Good morning! Anybody home?" Shauna's voice came from the kitchen as her daddy headed down the back stairway curious to see who had entered the back door. He had a sneaking suspicion it was his baby girl and he was long past due for a bear hug.

"Good morning, yourself!" He met her with a strong, comforting hug and a kiss on the cheek, just as he had done all of her life.

"I got in late last night and didn't want to disturb you, but when I discovered I didn't have any coffee this morning, I hurried over before I dressed." Pouring a cup, her eyes searched for the pink box of pastries she was hoping for, but nothing was in sight. As she lifted the cup to her lip, she pouted a little. "Any treats from Mockingbird Coffee House hidden in the pantry, by chance?"

He wore his coat, ready to head out the door, but waylaid a few minutes to chat. He leaned on the kitchen counter and reminded her of life in the Murphy house during the holidays. "Sorry, sweetie. You haven't been gone so long that you forgot that everyone fends for themselves this time of the year, have you? All of the focus is on selling Christmas."

Shauna rolled her eyes. "A girl can dream without sugar plums dancing in her head, can't she?"

Ryan Murphy knew all too well his daughter's disdain for the commercialism of Christmas and his wife's passion for the season. He grinned. "Not in this house. Sugar plums are required." He pointed at the candies in the canister on the countertop. "If you're still into your morning run, you can make the Mockingbird your 'go-to' morning stop. I told Ada you were coming. She would love to see you. They are ringing in the holiday with their specialty drinks. They've got me hooked on Peppermint Mocha. I drop in on the way to the shop every morning now." He patted his belly in proof. "Looks like you could add a couple of pounds."

"Stress is a great weight-loss plan. That's why I'm not too concerned with pastries. I've basically been nibbling or forget to eat until I'm reminded by the grumbling." Shauna sighed. Wanting to change the conversation, she pointed to the decorations.

"From the looks of things around here, somebody had time to decorate. The house looks amazing." Curiously she surveyed the simple theme her mother always chose. Understated but intricate details showed in the carved wooden nativity. No glitz or glitter would ever be found in the Murphy house. It was folk art at its best. Homespun decorations decked the stairwell; mantles and wreaths made from cedar, bitter-sweet, and holly leaves with berries. Candles were placed in the windows. It took you back to a simpler time. The only thing missing was the tree.

"Since your mom has added the 'In-Home Personal Christmas Decorating Service', the decorators swooped in the day after Halloween and transformed the house." He nodded his head in agreement as he glanced around. "It was hassle-free for me. I think this is the first time ever my hands weren't sticky from stringing pine rope."

She saw him glance over to the antique clock on the mantle. Realizing he was running late he said, "The guys have been putting in overtime to complete projects for the holidays. I have a new client that's stopping in this morning to check on the custom fireplace mantle I've crafted. It's a replica of an original from the early 1800s. It's incredible." She'd wondered why he was rushing off to work on Saturday morning.

Shauna always admired the way her father took pride in his work. He was an internationally known artisan for his Appalachian woodworking skills. Each piece was exquisite. Born and raised in the mountains, he learned his carpentry skills from his grandfather and father. The tradition of building furniture was passed on from generation to generation. In the early days, he built a regional business from traveling the craft circuit just to put food on the table. Over the years that expanded to an international business with custom-designed masterpieces that were exhibited in museums and mansions throughout the country. She had a hand in his international business. Being a social media marketing guru, she was proud that she'd helped her dad launch his online business that had sent his sales through the roof.

"Want to come with me? He's single." He raised his eyebrows and cocked his head.

"Really, Daddy?" She pointed to her snowmen pajamas. "Besides, don't you think it's a little early to be playing matchmaker?"

"Okay, okay." He threw his hands up in surrender and laughed.

"You better get out of here. Maybe we can order pizza tonight and catch up."

He complied, grabbed his keys from the kitchen drawer and started toward the door, but turned around. "Almost forgot, I want to show you a super-secret piece I'm working on. It's going to be amazing." He winked as he headed out the back door. "I love you, girl! I've missed you!" he exclaimed.

"Love you!" she returned.

That was one constant in their family. She always knew she was loved. She may have hated holidays and clashed with her mom's enchantment for Christmas, but love resided in their home. Parents are not supposed show favoritism, but she was more like her dad, and her sister was her mother's Mini-Me, so they naturally spent more time with those whose temperaments matched. She wondered about the big secret project. She despised secrets and he knew it.

#

Shauna found saltine crackers in the cupboard to help settle her stomach. Pouring one last cup of coffee before she dressed for the day, she felt the familiar greeting ritual of the family cat, rubbing against her ankle. Alice looked up with begging eyes and nudged her head a little harder, purring and meowed a greeting. Shauna reached down and scooped her up, lovingly stroking under her chin, as the purring grew louder. Alice was her comfort cat. In high school after a breakup, Gran adopted the calico beauty at the local animal shelter and brought her home one day as an impulsive gift. She turned out to be the best healer for the breakup. She was the perfect companion. With a 'no pet policy' in her new apartment in Atlanta, her parents offered to keep Alice to help her out, but she knew they didn't want to give up Alice, they had turned into "cat people."

Giving the bundle of fur a big squeeze, Shauna whispered, "I sure could have used my comfort cat."

Chapter Three

The doorbell rang, followed by someone banging relentlessly on the door calling out her name. Shauna didn't make it to the bakery. She didn't even make it to her suitcase for a change of clothes. She had fallen back to sleep all cozy on the couch in the cottage. It took her a second to realize where she was. It took longer for her feet to hit the floor. "Hang on. You're going to knock the wreath off." She answered the door still in her red snowmen pajamas, hoping it wasn't a tall, dark, and handsome stranger on the other side. It wasn't. It was her short, pale, and somewhat attractive sister who immediately started lecturing.

"I've been texting and calling you all morning. It's almost noon! Why haven't you picked up or answered my texts? I've been worried sick." Abby, being the older responsible sister and sometimes protector, came across a little bossy this morning, but Shauna didn't mind this time as she stood there with her arms outstretched greeting her guest.

She was a grown-up woman, but in her red

snowmen pajamas, tussled hair and goofy half-awake smile, Abby just saw her little sister as the toddler who would knock on her bedroom door, clutching a teddy bear, hoping her big sis would rescue her from the monster under her bed.

Abby held back when she realized Shauna needed a sympathetic shoulder not a sermon. The monster was back. This time it wasn't imaginary. Abby knew the last few months had been a major ordeal for her little sis. The sexual harassment from her slithering snake, stalker of a supervisor and the lawsuit that followed wreaked havoc on Shauna. If that wasn't enough, her so-called boyfriend, who she'd met at the office, decided it was best to *distance himself* from the situation and ended their relationship.

The special sister bond they shared had continued via their iPhones. They had spent hours talking and texting, but now seeing her eye-to-eye, woman-to-woman, Abby saw that Shauna hadn't been totally honest. She'd hidden her pain. She wasn't alright. *Dear God, help her.* Abby took the role of counselor and was determined not to let Shauna fall into a deep dark depression.

They embraced and held on tight. Her big sis gathered Shauna as a hen gathered a little chick, sheltering her under her protective wing. It felt good to be home.

Attempting to answer the original question, Shauna explained, "I'm on a 30-day social media detox. My therapist said I needed to set boundaries and it would help me deal with my stress." She longingly looked at her lonely iPhone lying on the coffee table with a black screen.

"Can't you just use it as a phone and not bother with social media?" Abby suggested.

"I'm following the recommended steps. I am on step four and turned it on airplane mode before I went to bed last night. I didn't get around to turning it back on this morning." She smiled. "I'm guessing that's a good sign."

Shauna walked like a zombie toward the couch.

"Don't even think about it!" Abby led Shauna by the arm toward the bedroom closet. "Sleep is overrated. I need your help."

"What's so important that I can't relax this morning? I'm tired," she moaned, hoping for a little sympathy.

"I had to take the twins with me to the store today. The sitter has this flu that's going around and Tyler had business out of town, so they're with me. It's crazy busy. They've been following Mom around like little elf helpers, but I think I've pushed themselves and Mom beyond their limits. They need a break. Plus, they want a little Auntie Shauna time."

"Now you're playing the guilt card." She kept walking toward the bedroom. "You're good – evil, but good."

Abby threw back her head and let out an evil laugh.

The familiar teasing made Shauna grin. "What's in it for me, besides kissing their faces off?"

"I'll take you for a quick bite for lunch at the Mockingbird. I know it's an offer you won't refuse."

"You got that right. Give me a couple of minutes." Remembering her clothes were still in her suitcase, she said, "Hope you don't mind wrinkles and a beanie to calm these crazy curls."

Shauna hurried and forgot about her worries for the first time in a long time.

#

"I hope we can get a table." Abby pulled into the last parking spot. They jumped out of the car and, arm in arm, walked down the snow-dusted sidewalk and headed toward the coffee house, a former 1871 Greek Revival house of worship, adorned with vaulted ceilings and soaring arches. The stained glass gave the converted coffee house a spiritual ambiance.

Escaping the cold, they burst in the door as the jingle sleigh bell, strapped on the handle, announced their entry. The intoxicating aroma of coffee blended with cinnamon, gingerbread, and peppermint announced the holiday season had arrived in full force. They quickly made their way to the line that was backed up at the ordering counter.

"Daddy said he was hooked on Peppermint Mocha." Shauna eyed the menu board. "What's your favorite?"

"I love the gingerbread latte, and the cutest mini gingerbread-man cookie is served on the side." Abby took in a deep breath of the sweet, buttery gingerbread goodness wafting in the air. "I think she just added the cookie so customers wouldn't try to eat the cup, wanting more."

"Hello, Ada!"

"Well, hello, girls!" The woman from behind the counter grinned. "You are a sight for sore eyes. Your dad said you were coming in. I've been on the lookout for you."

Everyone knew and loved Ada Taylor. She was a town treasure. Like other firsts in your life that make a lifelong impression, Ada was the first-grade teacher for almost every kid in the community. After retiring, she joined the little downtown business community and pursued her dream of opening a coffee house and purchased a historic church building. It miraculously came on the market, which was appropriate, since Ada also claimed the title of the First Lady of the AME Zion Church. Ada was known for her traditional Appalachian holiday desserts, especially the Hummingbird Cake, but what really drew people to her coffee house was her listening ear and tender heart. You could count on a friendly personal greeting upon arrival and a *God bless you*, when you departed. Those words that parted her lips were as natural as breathing to Ada. And just in case she missed you when you entered, there was a scripture plaque over the door that read, *The LORD bless thee, and keep thee.*

She knew most by their first name and the townspeople called a visit to the Mockingbird "coffee therapy." Who needed a therapist when Ada not only served the best coffee and dessert in town, but was the best listener in the world who locked away secrets and threw away the key? Plus, unbeknownst to her customers, Ada was a prayer whisperer. Every cup of coffee was topped off with a silent blessing of mercy and grace.

The place was too busy to chit chat, so the sisters placed their order and Ada advised, "Better grab a table up in the balcony. I think there's one left beside the Giving Tree. I'll bring your order out to you, ASAP, personally."

They made their way up the grand entrance stairway, draped with festive green winter garland, and found the empty table. The sweet sound of the Appalachian dulcimer playing carols in the background added to the festive atmosphere. They unbundled and settled in their seats beside the decorated tree. Abby excused herself for a quick trip to the ladies' room and left Shauna alone with her thoughts. As she looked around the jammed-packed coffee house, she observed a group of ladies, probably on a lunch break, chattering away like the hens that woke her just a few hours earlier. One woman's voice stood out over the others and occasionally cackled out an ear-piercing laugh, enjoying time with friends.

Shauna used to have work friends like that, until she didn't. Looking away from the reminders of her hurt, her eyes found a cozy couple all snuggled up in a tiny booth, sipping their hot chocolate, deep in conversation. Loneliness and loss surfaced quickly, breaking through the barricade she'd built around her heart. Emotions were an invisible, silent enemy that she hadn't conquered – yet. She'd tried denial. It revolted against her when physical symptoms of emotional trauma flared up. The bombardment of a constant pit in her stomach, anxiety, panic attacks, headaches, and lethargy, caused her to surrender to therapy.

Her therapist said she was experiencing signs of post-traumatic stress disorder. That little secret she kept to herself. She was embarrassed to be perceived as weak. Her daddy always said she was *courageous and strong willed.* She clung to those words during the nightmare of being sexual harassed. *She was courageous. She was strong.* She succeeded in the lawsuit. *She was courageous. She was strong.* But she underestimated the tsunami of the toxic, hidden effects that violently flooded over, wave after wave. *She was afraid. She was weak.* With the guidance of her therapist, she was beginning to recognize the warning signs. *She was courageous. She was strong.* Abby was good at sending her scripture texts to encourage her, she remembered a recent verse from Proverbs: *Be brave, be strong. Don't give up. God will be here soon.* She wondered what He was waiting for.

Returning from the ladies' room, Abby saw Shauna. She was lost in thought, twirling a long lock of hair, twisting tighter and tighter. She realized maybe she had taken too long.

"Sorry I took so long. I ran into the photographer organizing the pictures with Santa at the Train Depot, she asked if we could provide a few more decorations for the photo ops."

"That's okay," Shauna said. Wanting to take her mind to a better place, she asked, "What's this Giving Tree all about?" Shauna gazed at the tree dotted with an eclectic variety of ornaments, tied to the branch with colorful ribbon.

"Ada started this little tradition a couple of years ago. Anyone in the community can fill out a request and tie the little scroll on an ornament. The uniqueness of The Giving Tree is the wish cannot be for you or an immediate family member."

"That's an interesting concept."

"It gets more interesting. The volunteers who take the request cannot accomplish it by themselves. They can only facilitate. First, they are paired up with another volunteer, then they have to recruit others to help make the hopeful wishes come true."

"That's crazy cool!" Shauna's mind immediately thought of social media networks and how quickly things multiply and spread across them. "It would get so many more people involved in helping others instead of just one individual writing a big fat check."

"Yep, it's all about getting the whole community onboard."

As Ada made her way to the table with a full tray in hand, she saw them admiring the tree.

"Here you go, girls."

"Oh, my gosh, this looks amazing!" Shauna's eyes brightened as she ogled Ada's Hummingbird cake, secretly hoping, if her stomach allowed, she would be able to eat the entire meal. But, just in case, she decided to start with dessert. The aroma of the magical blend of banana, pineapple, and spice was heavenly. It was all she could do not to face plant in the cake.

"I wish I could sit and chat, but it's really busy," said Ada. "Please drop by when it's a little slower so we can catch up." Looking at Shauna, she said, "I saw you checking out my little ornaments of hope. I would love for you to volunteer. The kickoff for the Giving Tree is tomorrow night at seven. There's nothing like a little hope to get you in the Christmas spirit."

Shauna wasn't really trying to get in the Christmas spirit, but she did need some hope. She agreed to come.

Gossiping and eating were two of Abby's favorite sports. She suddenly stopped mid-sentence, and directed her attention across the balcony.

"Hey, Gabe, come on over, I want to introduce you to my baby sister."

The excited gleam in Abby's eye worried

Shauna. Shauna understood that gleam when she turned to see the man walking toward their table. He was wonderful to look at. He was tall and his shoulders were broad. His face held a square jaw and stubble. Thick and wavy, his hair looked tousled, and she had to admit, a little sexy. And his eyes, a deep hazel, were warm and kind.

Shauna smiled. Gabe reached out his hand as Shauna quickly sat down her coffee mug to extend hers.

"Gabe, this is my sister Shauna. She's in town for the holidays." Abby secretly hoped it would be more than just the holidays.

"Pleasure to meet you, Shauna."

"Nice meeting you." His touch sent an unexpected sensation through her arm.

Abby continued. "You've actually met before."

Apologetic, Shauna said, "I don't think so, but it's been a while since I've been home."

"Gabe is the new owner of the Spring Valley Inn, but we met him a long time ago."

"That's right," Gabe said, agreeing. "That was a long, long time ago."

Abby kept the conversation moving, reminding Shauna. "Remember when we took that white-water rafting trip the first summer after your freshman year in college?"

Abby recalled her one and only white-water rafting trip. "Yes, the one I didn't think I would ever live to remember. Who could forget? I almost drowned."

"I think you're being a little bit of a drama queen," Abby quibbled.

Gabe looked on, admiring the playful banter between sisters. As an only child he always wondered what he'd missed out on.

Hearing laughter, while going from table to table refilling coffee mugs, Ada stretched her neck in the direction of Gabe and the girls, watching curiously. A grin spread over her face as she whispered, *"Lord, bless them"* and her eyes got that familiar matchmaking twinkle. She was always willing to do the Lord's work.

"The way I remember it, everyone begged me to go, 'to venture out on the wild side and try an exhilarating experience'. All I recall was being terrified and screaming, as we bounced down the river over rough waves, paddling at the speed of sound, dodging humongous killer rocks and being drenched to the bone," said Shauna, though she and Abby were both laughing. "After we landed on dry land, I kissed the ground."

"Surely it wasn't that frightening. That sounds fun to me," Gabe chimed in. "As a guide I've never lost anyone to the river." Shauna detected a hint of a Boston accent as he dropped the final 'r' in river.

Pointing at Gabe, Abby said, "He was our guide that day. Tyler and I were planning a trip for last summer and found out Gabe was into white-water rafting. After swapping rafting stories, we determined he was our guide back then." As the words left her lips, Abby thought that maybe it hadn't been just a coincidence but a *Godincidence.*

As Shauna looked at Gabe, his long-lost image came rushing back to her mind. She recalled this ruggedly handsome guide all decked out in a wetsuit at the helm of the raft. After returning home, his image had lingered in her mind, tempting her to try rafting one more time. She distinctly remembered almost giving in to the temptation, crossing her fingers in hope for the same handsome guide and maybe a summer romance. But, ultimately, she thought of the death-defying experience and chose life over a slim chance of romance and checked it off her been-there-done-that list.

Gabe interrupted her thoughts. "You'll have to give it another try this summer. Don't let one bad experience ruin it for you. If you put a little faith in me, I promise, I'll protect you."

Something told her, he spoke the truth.

Chapter Four

Gabe Anderson stepped out into the cold, crisp air, leaving the coffee house, somewhat surprised he'd enjoyed his brief encounter with Shauna. Three years had passed since his newlywed wife succumbed to cancer. He hadn't looked twice at another woman since. Without Robin, he felt as if he had stopped living the day she drew her last breath. Maybe the little flutter his heart had experienced was the first sign of life.

It wasn't because he hadn't had enough encouragement to date, he just had too many other pressing matters to think about romance. It seemed as if everyone in town wanted to *fix him up*. Unbeknownst to him, someone even crossed the line and set up a Match.com profile. When the dating-profile gossip spread like wildfire, he didn't think it too funny when a friend congratulated him on *getting out there*. It was still a mystery who posted the profile, but after he voiced his displeasure it quickly came down.

"Merry Christmas, Gabe!" One of his downtown neighbors, hanging a window wreath, paused to send a holiday hello.

"Hello, Mrs. Barkley!" Lost in thought, he didn't see her standing on the tall ladder. "Hold on, I'll steady the ladder for you." He considered her age and added, "Better yet, come down and let me hang it for you."

"That would be nice of you. I forget sometimes how old I am until these aching bones remind me," she bemoaned, as she slowly navigated the slender steps. "Mr. Barkley is under the weather and I just thought the house needed a little holiday sprucing up. I didn't want to be the only house on Main Street without any decorations." Finding her footing on the sidewalk, she inquired, "How are the repairs going?"

"Things have slowed a little with the holidays, but I'm hoping to reopen by mid-January," he replied, as he placed the wreath with care, making sure it was centered because Mrs. Barkley would let him know the error of his decorating skills.

"I wish you the best of luck," she said, while crossing her fingers, "hopefully you'll fill all the rooms for Valentine's weekend."

Gabe noticed a pile of wreaths on the porch, and suggested, "How about letting me hang those wreaths? I'm assuming they go on all the windows."

"Oh, that would be wonderful!" She clapped her hands in approval. "You are an angel!"

Mrs. Barkley slowly shuffled over to fetch the wreaths and handed them to him one-by-one, as they finished the task together. With rosy cheeks and a sniffling nose, Mrs. Barkley bid him farewell and joined her husband inside for a warm cup of tea. Gabe worried she had been out in the cold for too long. He made a mental note to check on her tomorrow. The Barkleys were both in their late seventies and an independent couple, especially Mrs. Barkley. She was determined to live out their days in their home and didn't want anyone to think otherwise. He knew that Mr. Barkley was more than just "under the weather." He displayed signs of Alzheimer's, which they both knew, but they didn't want to face life without the other. In hope against hope, they believed God would answer their daily prayer of just one more day together. Since their daughter lived out of state, she'd lined up an in-home care service to check in on them a couple of times a week, to help with light housekeeping, run errands, and grocery shopping. She also gave Gabe her phone number in case of an emergency. He would concoct a reason for a neighborly visit, so Mrs. Barkley wouldn't think he was an informer. He was a strong believer in the scripture, *Love your neighbor as you love yourself.*

Gabe didn't mind the interruption. He felt fortunate that a small town would adopt a stranger into the fold so easily. Especially a Northerner. Everyone treated him like family, now. He and Robin Martin met in college in New Hampshire, where his mother was an instructor. Spring graduation was followed by a June wedding and a whirlwind move to Tennessee to manage Robin's grandparents' historic inn. Robin and Gabe had spent their whole lives in the northeast but were both linked to the South through relatives. In high school, Gabe's Aunt Alana relocated to Asheville for work at the Biltmore Inn. After he and his mom made their first tip to visit, he was hooked. The beauty of the mountains and outdoor adventures guaranteed extended summer stays. Robin spent her summers and holidays in Spring Valley working in her grandparents' little historic inn, which she loved, and eventually hospitality became her career path. She earned a Hospitality Management degree and wanted to spend quality time with her aging grandparents. Gabe loved the majestic mountains, hiking, camping, but most of all, he loved Robin, so it was a win-win situation for both. His Business Administration degree would be an asset and he decided he could learn hospitality management hands-on. They settled in as innkeepers, but only after a few months, Robin's beloved grandparents, within days apart, died. They left the inn and a small inheritance to their only grandchild.

Robin decided to use a portion of her inheritance to breathe new life into the outdated property. Booking an historic inn didn't necessarily mean vacationers wanted to step back in time and abandon technology or creature comforts. Her degree in hospitality gave her a strong foundation, but during the first few weeks managing the inn, she learned first-hand that guests have high expectations and if they wanted to continue wooing weary travelers, they had to upgrade. The budget didn't allow them to strip it to its skeleton, but it was enough to give the inn a twenty-first-century upgrade. She was careful to keep the historic character of the inn. She added the latest technology with Wi-Fi, on-demand TV, and a customized security system. Each room was refreshed and redecorated to give a touch of elegance, and beds were dressed in luxurious linens. Capitalizing on the trend of destination weddings, she hired a landscape artist to design a charming English garden overflowing with plants and lush flowers that led to a magical gate and courtyard. It was perfect for an intimate, romantic wedding venue. Robin was thrilled with the new renovations and, more importantly, she carried on her grandparents' legacy.

Inn keeping was second nature for Robin, but Gabe grew into his role of innkeeper. It suited him. There were pros and cons to a married couple working together but they seemed to balance the scale on the pro side. They acclimated to being newlyweds and innkeepers like a seasoned married couple. The investment paid off when bookings increased after the renovations, but their lives were demolished with the devastating diagnosis of Robin's stage IV breast cancer. The disease took over their lives as the cancer spread quickly to her liver, lungs, and bones. They spent more time in hospitals than they did at the inn. She didn't survive. He held her funeral days after their second wedding anniversary. Spring Valley Inn was now a legacy left by Robin for Gabe to carry on.

Standing at the entrance to the inn, Gabe stood in amazement that it had withstood the test of time. Built in the late 1790s, over the centuries the inn had welcomed weary travelers, who first came by stage coach or horse and buggy that had navigated the rutted, muddy streets. Just a block over from the railroad depot, the inn served as a respite for traveling doctors, lawyers, soldiers, peddlers, and politicians. The mud gave way to flagstone streets, and eventually asphalt for cars. The ever-present danger of fire always lurked in the shadows. Spring Valley Inn was the only wooden building still standing after a fire almost demolished the town in the late 1800s. Three years after he lost Robin, devastation hit again, and he came close to losing the inn to a kitchen fire. Fortunately, history repeated itself and the inn survived, but Gabe had to temporarily close right after Halloween for repairs. With the month-long Christmas festivities, this was usually a busy time for the inn. He was forced to cancel reservations, which definitely put a damper on the season. He hoped and prayed the upcoming festivities would jump start a merry mood.

#

Walking hand in hand with her niece and nephew Shauna felt as if she stepped back to a simpler time. Remarkably, she might still have been that little girl walking the snow-dusted brick side-walks, securely holding her Gran's hand, going from store to store seeking the perfect one-of-a-kind Christmas gift to place under the tree.

Atlanta's crazy crowds filled the busy streets, malls, and hectic fashion district that offered jaw-dropping apparel and all the must-have tech gadgets. Spring Valley had its own holi-day magic. The atmosphere was reminiscent of a simple old-fashioned Christmas with charming artisan shops and galleries selling some of the finest Appalachian folk art you can find in the South. It was where traditions of old were kept alive and passed on to the next generation. Work-ing artists displayed their handcrafted gifts with a collection of chain sawed cedar Christmas trees, wooden snowmen, sculptured and fabric Santa dolls, glass-blown ornaments, and nativity scenes made with gourds and corn husk. As she held her niece and nephew's little mittened hands she re-gretted missing the last few Christmases in Spring Valley. Shauna thought just maybe the therapist was right – she needed to reconnect to her past to find her future.

"Here it is! Here it is, Auntie Shauna." With unison cries out in wonder, the twins tugged her toward the candy store.

"Of course, this is where you wanted to go,"

Shauna teased, "and I thought you wanted to shop for presents for your mommy and daddy."

A giant teddy bear greeted them at the door of the Old-Timey Sweet Shop. They made a beeline straight to the jumbo-sized gumdrops in a clear glass jar on the counter. Shauna remembered those soft, chewy mouthfuls of joy as Paige and Bryce singled out their favorite flavor.

"Guess what was my favorite flavor when I was a little girl."

"Watermelon!" Paige guessed.

"No. Bryce, you guess."

"Pineapple, because you like Hawaii."

"Good guess, Bryce, I do love Hawaii, but my favorite is spiced cinnamon." Shauna pointed over to the spiced gumdrop jar.

"Yuck!' They expressed their disgust.

"I want cherry!" Bryce declared.

"I want orange, no... lemon." Paige had trouble choosing.

"What do you say?" Shauna prompted them.

"Please and thank you!" They held out their hands, waiting for a tasty goody.

The dentist in town probably loathed the store owner who handed out a free humongous gum drop to any kid who set foot in his store. He was a marketing genius. *Free of charge* equaled *purchase of sale*. Straightaway, they held their sugary treat in their hands and grabbed a bag to fill with old-time candy – in bulk.

Shauna had several hours to fill before returning the kids to Abby, so they made their way to her daddy's woodworking shop. It was only a few blocks away and the kids were up for an adventure to see their Papaw Ryan. Before entering the doorway, Shauna bent down to wipe the sticky sugar off the kids' hands. Exquisite furniture and sticky hands make a bad combination. Just as she raised her head the door opened and slightly bumped her noggin, which made the chivalrous gesture a little awkward.

"I am so sorry. Are you alright?" Gabe reached out a strong arm to steady her balance as she stumbled backward.

Shauna was rattled and rubbing her forehead, looked up to see a familiar face. "We meet again." She smiled, then teasing him said, "I thought you said you protected people. Should I wear a helmet the next time we meet?"

The twins giggled as they watched Gabe continue to hold their auntie close as she recovered her balance.

The look in Gabe's eyes gave away his concern and embarrassment.

Shauna laughed, hoping to put his mind to rest. "I'm fine, I'm just teasing you. It was barely a scrape. That's when a wooly beanie and thick curly hair serve as a stand-in helmet."

He was befuddled by the moment of attraction he felt. "Again, I'm so sorry. Let me do this properly." He held the door for them, hoping she didn't think he was clumsy, *and* a sexist for holding the door open. But it was the least he could do.

Shauna was surprised this Southern tradition came from a Northerner. She was independent, but since she was raised in the South, it didn't bother her, like it did some of her friends who didn't like doors opened for them. As they entered, Shauna smiled and thanked him. She tried not to make too much eye contact with Gabe, as her cheeks were flushed. She didn't want to give away the surprising effect he seemed to have on her.

She passed so close he could smell the season in her hair. He wondered if the aroma of vanilla mixed with sugar and spice was an intentional holiday selection. It was nice. It matched her personality. It was one of those delicious fragrances that smelled good enough to eat. Lingering in the air, it put a sumptuous rumble in his stomach. Pulling up his coat around his chin to shield from the chill, Gabe shook his head in embarrassment. Or was it the spontaneous palpable pull that embarrassed him?

Still flustered, Shauna felt her Gran whispering her romantic ideals to her: *A man who holds the door for a lady is probably a keeper.*

#

The smell of ash-wood shavings and the tiny particles of sawdust that floated in the air brought on an immediate sneeze, which forced Shauna back to the present. Several of the workers removed their dust masks and responded together,

"God bless you." One of the guys yelled out in disappointment, "You just killed another fairy." Never having heard the folklore that if you say "bless you" after a sneeze, a fairy dies; Shauna's niece and nephew were both confused and horrified by the thought of the demise of a sweet little fairy. Shauna assured them that the Tooth Fairy was alive and well and not to worry. She made her rounds, greeting the artisans who paused long enough to give her a welcome-home hug. They had watched Shauna mature into a beautiful young woman. She considered them family. She was part of theirs.

"I see you met Gabe," her daddy said, "he's the new 'single' client I told you about this morning." He smiled inquisitively.

"Yes, that's the second time today, we literally ran into each other." Shauna watched the kids head to the warmth of the wood-heated stove. Her dad corralled them in his office, where he kept toys and snacks for them to occupy their time, so he could show off his handiwork.

"This is the fireplace mantle Gabe commissioned." As he walked toward the exquisite mantle with its smooth finished curves, tapered columns, and richly detailed, ornate carvings he could hardly wait to show her. All of his projects were a labor of love.

"This is amazing, Daddy. Was he pleased?"

"He loved it. We should be able to deliver next week, after the contractor's painting is complete." He flashed her another grin. "Want to make the delivery with me?"

"I don't know, maybe. But I do know that between you and Abby, I think I'm doomed," Shauna conceded and changed the conversation. "Where's that top-secret project you're working on?"

"It's in the back. Let me make sure the grandkids are distracted. They can't see this."

That piqued Shauna's interest. What in the world was he crafting that was for adults' eyes only? As he uncovered the piece, she was caught off guard and questioned her dad. "You're making coffins, now?"

"It's not advertised, but I've had a few special requests." He grabbed a few pictures to show Shauna his handy work. "This first coffin wasn't as ornate as the one I'm working on now."

She saw a pic of a replica of Pope John Paul II's cypress-wood coffin with a cross carved on the top. As she flipped through the pictures, the next was a project for a local man with Cherokee ancestry who'd commissioned a cedar-wood coffin painted in tribal colors, lined with an Indian blanket, and carved on the lid were ancestral symbols of feathers, an owl, and cougar.

As she gazed upon her father's new project in astonishment, she understood why the kids weren't allowed to see it. She warned him, "No, Daddy. No, no, no. You can't be known as the man who buried Santa Claus." She ran her hand over the cherry wood, deep-burgundy stained coffin, a replica of the nineteenth century coffins that taper toward the feet. It was adorned with carved Christmas images of trees, ornaments, and toys on the sides; with a carved Santa sleigh on the lid. The lining was red satin, trimmed with white fur. It was a masterpiece!

She burst out laughing. "Really, Daddy?"

"How could I turn Santa down?"

She knew he couldn't. The local Santa was not only the town's stand-in for the most beloved Father Christmas, he was one of her dad's closest friends.

"I'm pretty sure he's not planning on using this in the near future. So, where's he going to store it? Because this can't be his storehouse." She gestured in a wide swoop of his workshop.

"He's got room in his basement. Or, knowing him, he may use it as his dining table."

"Are you really considering adding custom coffins?" Shauna started brainstorming on how to market the concept in a serious and tasteful way. How would she convey that everyone is unique and their life mattered? It made her contemplate her choice for a custom-made coffin. She didn't know, and that troubled her. She felt her life meaningless, these days. It was ironic that a funerary box would point her thoughts to living. She hoped to find purpose somewhere in this detour of her life.

"They are very lucrative. Plus, I think they serve as a special memorial for those left behind.

The custom coffin seems to give comfort in the grieving process. It also allows a person to decide how they want to be remembered and interned in their final resting place." He knew it would take Shauna's skills to market these unique pieces. "Do you think you could design a marketing plan?"

"Challenge accepted! I've got time on my hands."

She could tell this was another way her daddy could express himself and his passion for woodworking. She imagined it would definitely be a conversation starter at funerals as they talked about their loved one and their life's passion. She started warming up to the concept. But even though she wasn't crazy about Christmas, she really didn't like the idea of her dad being known on social media as the guy who entombed Santa.

Chapter Five

Ada started her Sundays by 5 a.m. This Sunday morning she needed a little extra time and assistance from her husband before he left for church. She snagged the Reverend Joshua Robert Taylor on his way to the coffee maker, and had him sit at the kitchen table to draw names out of a box that would pair volunteers for the Giving Tree project. He noticed a couple of stray cards on the counter and stretched over to gather and throw them in the box.

"Leave those alone. I have plans for those two." Ada brushed his hand away.

J.R. ignored her and read the names of Shauna Murphy and Gabe Anderson.

"Ada, what are you up to? This is supposed to be a random drawing." He directed a scolding eye to his wife.

She gave him a guilty look. "Sometimes the good Lord uses me as his emissary. And you know that I've never been one to turn down His mission."

After forty anniversaries, he knew there was no use in trying to derail one of his wife's *missions*.

He shook his head. "Do they have any idea you're their designated guardian angel or, should I say, their Cupid?"

She placed a playful kiss on his forehead. "Not a clue!"

He grabbed his Bible and flew out the door before she asked for another favor. "Don't be late!"

"I've never been late for church a day in my life, and you know it." She blew him a kiss as her voice trailed behind him.

Ada had thought about adding a counseling room in the back of the coffee house, since everybody wanted to tell her their problems, but the bistro tables seemed to work just fine. A smile and a cup of coffee tended to open the floodgates, plus she was always willing to listen and stir a little wisdom into the brew. She had to admit that on more than one occasion she was guilty of playing matchmaker. It turned out to be a favorite hobby. She could give Match.com a run for their money. She and J.R. were childless, but she felt blessed having a part in helping raise kids in her classroom. While J.R. ministered at the AME Zion Church, she considered her classroom a calling to shepherd her little flock. After retirement she felt her café was a divine calling as well. After all, her desserts were called *heavenly*.

Spring Valley wasn't the most diverse community but Ada and J.R. both had roots that went way back – as far as the late 1700s when the pioneers settled in the foothills of the Appalachian

Mountains, and brought their slaves with them. She never really wanted to move away. She was sentimental and heritage meant more than a list of names written in the front of a family Bible. She was proud of the culture of her mountain roots, or, as they now say, her Affrilachian roots. She even had ancestors buried in the old cemetery on the hill, where the town's founding fathers were buried. She knew history books didn't mention her ancestors as "founding fathers." considering they were slaves, but they toiled the ground alongside their owners, laid bricks, built their homes, cooked their food, sewed their dresses, cleaned their homes, and raised their children. They buried them as they lived – in separate quarters – but even though they may have been separated by a ditch that divided the cemetery, she knew they all had one thing in common, whether black or white: they had all met their Maker. And meeting her Maker was the guiding factor in Ada's life. Over the years, in spite of discrimination, she broke out of the tendency to see in black and white. Ada was color-blind and felt a calling to meet and minister to the interest of others, no matter their color. She was convinced that we were all of God's children, and the doctrine of *love conquers hate* could bring an end to racial divides. She was an enthusiastic disciple.

Ada was blessed with the chance for success when she received a scholarship to Berea College in Kentucky. Berea was founded as an abolitionist college that welcomed black and white men and women students from the Appalachian region. They welcomed her with open arms. Their scripture motto through the years was, *God has made of one blood all peoples on the earth*. Berea College wasn't her plan. Her senior year of high school, her English teacher secretly sent in an application for Ada. When she was accepted everyone was so excited for the opportunity, except for Ada. She was apprehensive to leave J. R., her childhood sweetheart, and her family to face the unknown world, but God had a plan. It was there she obtained her teaching degree and also her passion for cooking. Like all her fellow students, she worked in the Labor Program, earning money to help pay her educational expenses. The opportunity to work with the sous-chef at the historic Boone Tavern contributed to her culinary skills and her second career at the Mockingbird Coffee House. God used a teacher's act of kindness and ability to see a future greater than Ada could ever imagine. It transformed her life. Ada's life motto became based on the scripture, Jeremiah 29:11, *For I know the plans that I have for you, declares the Lord, plans for welfare and not for calamity to give you a future and a hope.*

Her gratitude turned into a lifetime of giving. She dedicated her life to paying it forward, always listening and obeying God's whispers. She became a devout emissary of hope.

#

Shauna timed her late arrival so she wouldn't have

to stop and chat with everyone she knew. Her mistake was not remembering the Giving Tree was stationed in the loft, which meant all eyes would be on her as she made her tardy grand entrance at the top of the stairs. So much for sneaking in.

"Sorry, I'm late," Shauna murmured her apology toward Ada as she made a beeline for the complimentary coffee on a reception table. She smiled and, in fun, gestured a beauty-queen wave to the cheerful-looking group. As anticipated, they laughed in amusement. Finding a seat in the crowded room, she thought it might have been simpler if she had ignored Ada's invitation and just stayed home.

Getting comfy, she saw across the room the now familiar, irresistibly attractive face of Gabe Anderson. They stared at each other – maybe a little longer than they each intended. Gabe smiled and nodded a hello her way. Shauna held his gaze for a moment, smiled and turned her attention to Ada, but her thoughts were still on the man. Frustrated with her thoughts, she didn't know what had gotten into her. She was still mending from a broken heart, and a traumatic experience. Her trust meter on men was stuck at zero. However, she did wonder if any of the women at his table were in his companionship. For some mystified reason, she hoped not.

Ada was talking, but for a moment, Gabe didn't hear her. His mind was still on Shauna and he'd observed that her beauty-queen wave seemed instinctive. He wondered if her natural cinnamon curls that cascaded over her shoulders had ever held a crown – if they had not, they should have.

Ada noticed the stolen glances, as did her husband, J.R. Nonchalantly, as Ada addressed the crowd, she turned toward J.R. with a little raised eyebrow and gave him the *I told you so* look that he knew well. He sat back and watched as she so gracefully went about her *Father's business*.

"I want to thank all of you for coming tonight," Ada gleefully greeted her guests. "Before we distribute the ornaments and pair up volunteers, I wanted to share a scripture with you. I know that this time of year you expect the nativity scripture, but these words leaped off the page during my morning devotional." She affectionately gestured toward her husband and continued. "J.R. is the preacher in our family and I know you didn't come to hear me preach, but..."

Someone in the audience yelled, "Go ahead, preach it Ada."

Everyone laughed and she replied, "Whomever that was, you get a free cup of coffee tonight."

"I thought the coffee was already free, tonight."

The audience roared again.

"Anyways, all kidding aside, just bear with me for a minute because I think this is so apropos for Spring Valley and our Giving Tree project."

She began reading Isaiah 58:9-12 : *"If you*

get rid of unfair practices, quit blaming victims, quit gossiping about other people's sons, if you are generous with the hungry and start giving yourselves to the down-and-out, your lives will begin to glow in the darkness, your shadowed lives will be bathed in sunlight. I will always show you where to go. I'll give you a full life in the emptiest of places – firm muscles, strong bones. You will be like a well-watered garden, a gurgling spring that never runs dry. You'll use the old rubble of past lives to build anew, rebuild the foundations from out of your past. You'll be known as those who can fix anything, restore old ruins, rebuild, and renovate, make the community livable again."

The cheerful and rowdy group became quiet and reflective. Heads nodded in agreement as they listened reverently.

"The spring that lies a few blocks over led to the settlement of our town, Spring Valley. It has never run dry and has generously provided a life-giving water source for generations." Ada definitely felt like she was preaching. Her audience listened intently. "Our townspeople are known for generosity. Many of you have been a recipient of their open hands. This tree and all of these ornaments of hope represent people who, just like the scripture reads, *are hungry and down-and-out, needing hope for the future*." Pointing to the tree, she continued. "Tonight, you will glow in the darkness as you begin your quest to fulfill these Christmas wishes."

Her sermonette was received with a spontaneous and enthusiastic applause. She caught a few digging in their purse for tissues to blot away the tears.

Ada continued about her duty explaining the rules and then called out the names of the randomly drawn teammates. Halfway through, Shauna and Gabe miraculously became a couple.

Chapter Six

Tonight, the Mockingbird felt more like a church than a coffee house. Ada was overjoyed with the standing-room-only turnout that exceeded that of the previous year. The needs also surpassed last year's, as more ornaments trimmed the tree with little notes for Christmas wishes. She was so thankful for this small but mighty army of generous volunteers. She whispered a prayer: "Thank you, Lord – thank you, Jesus."

She reflected on how this beautiful historical church building, in one way or another, had hosted 147 Christmas celebrations. First as a church, then a lecture hall, a restaurant, a wedding venue and now her coffee house. One thing she knew for sure: when the congregation literally died out in the cholera pandemic of 1873, the spirit of the church lived on and never left the building. It may have slept for many years, but tonight it awoke, and sparked a movement of generosity.

\#

Hearing their names together, Shauna almost

spewed her coffee across the table. Why couldn't she be teamed up with a nice little old lady. *What was she thinking?* Her Gran answered in her thoughts as Shauna remembered what she'd always recited: *In helping others, you help yourself.*

Pleasantly surprised, Gabe raised his coffee mug to Shauna in an imaginary toast. He had hoped this altruistic act of volunteering for the Giving Tree would add some merry to his mood – he got his wish. He felt an immediate boost in his Christmas spirit. But he had to admit, Shauna wasn't on his wish list. He had no musings about Shauna, they had only just met, but he hoped that this might be a season of miracles after all. He recalled Francis of Assisi's words: *For it is in the giving that we receive.*

After Ada finished with the team announcements, it became Fruit Basket Upset as everyone arose and searched for their fellow wish-granter. Finally, alone at his table, Gabe's eyes wandered to Shauna and gestured for her to join him. She wasn't keen on taking orders, so instead, she shook her head in disagreement and like Vanna White, revealing letters on the *Wheel of Fortune*, with a sweeping gesture she revealed an empty chair at her table. She looked just as glamourous as Vanna and Gabe decided to go with the flow and joined her.

Ada never had a problem with starting a conversation, but she knew it could be awkward for others. She wanted her volunteers to get to know one another and feel comfortable before they started planning, so she'd placed a list of "Christmas Conversation Starters" on each table. She gave them ten minutes to chat and then they would move on to the ornaments.

With the dread of answering predictable questions, Shauna reached for the list and began reading. With a glance, she studied Gabe's face for any apprehension. He was calm and comfortable. In response to it, her anxiety calmed – a little.

"Just so you know, I like short answers," she told him with a teasing grin. "We don't need a dissertation. Think a tweet in 280 characters or less. That's give or take about fifty-five words or less."

"What if I don't tweet?"

He surprised her with that one. Shauna lived in the land of tweets and couldn't imagine a business owner in today's world not using Twitter. "You're kidding, right?" She looked at him in amazement.

"No, I find it too noisy. It clutters my mind."

She thought he sounded a lot like her therapist, but didn't share that tidbit of information.

"Wow, evidently you're not aware that I work in that world."

There were a lot of things he didn't know about her, and he wanted to get more acquainted. "Tell me more."

He mystified her by grinning. Was he teasing or goading her for more information? Surely her dad had blabbed about his baby girl. He had a tendency to brag. Either way, she thought she would enlighten him that he was lucky she was his teammate. "I'm in social media marketing. If you want to rocket your business to success through Facebook, Instagram, Twitter, or any other social media platform – I'm your girl."

"Good to know." Gabe was still caught on the phrase "I'm your girl."

"I think we can definitely use social media to help us with our project," she said. It was evident she didn't have to request short answers, he was the strong silent type. Her mind questioned what was hidden behind those strangely dreamy eyes. But she wasn't a fan of awkward silence and prodded, "Well, let's get these Christmas Conversation Starters going or Ada will call us out."

"Number one: What was Christmas like growing up?" asked Shauna.

Shauna laughed out loud. "This is an easy one. I'll go first. It was like every other day of the year. Since my mom owned a year-round Christmas store, the spirit of Christmas glowed the whole year through at our house."

"I get a sense that you're not a fan."

"Mom wrapped every day in Christmas. She even named me Shauna, it means 'present' in Celtic, because I was born on January six, the Old Christmas day celebrated in the mountains." With a dose of sarcasm, she added, "According to Appalachian folklore, a January sixth baby has special healing powers." Embarrassed she'd exceeded her fifty-five word count she encouraged Gabe, "Now, it's your turn."

Perhaps, he mused, he needed more healing and God had placed Shauna in his path. He didn't know if he believed in divine appointments, but from the first moment they met, he sensed something rare about Shauna. After Robin had died, his survival instinct took over. Shielding himself from future pain and suffering, he slammed the door shut on his heart, but now, he felt it, ever so slightly – open.

"Let's see, where to begin. I was raised by a single mom, so our Christmases didn't always look like the other kids on the block's did. But no matter if I had ten presents under the tree or one; mom always made it magical." Gabe tenderly spoke of his mother. Teasing Shauna, he said, "I think my word count is up... next."

Feeling a little guilty for complaining about her crazy Christmas life and her nuclear family, she continued. "Number two: Describe a favorite Christmas from your past." Shauna recalled a Christmas gone by. "That would be when I was ten years old and we were snowed in at my grandparents' house, tucked back in the mountains. We arrived Christmas morning, and by early afternoon, a snow blizzard blanketed the mountain with a foot of shimmering snow. I felt like Lucy in *The Chronicles of Narnia,* who stepped through a wardrobe that led to a fantasy winter world. Abby and I ventured out of the cabin in search of

Father Christmas, but it didn't last very long. The adventure wore off quickly and we returned like frosted snowmen. But we were certain we caught a glimpse of him in the woods."

Gabe leaned in. "I'll match you with a winter woods story. We moved from Boston to Manchester, New Hampshire when I was about ten. I fell in love with White Mountain and begged for a Christmas camping trip as a gift, never imagining Mom would give in. At that time, she was a sous-chef at a small restaurant. Usually, she would have had to work on the holiday, but they gave her the time off. Early on Christmas Eve, she pulled up in the driveway, in a camper van, with a friend of mine in the passenger seat. He was in on the surprise. His mom had to work during the holiday and was glad to find someone to look after him." Gabe ventured off, explaining. "Anyways, secretly, Mom had loaded up the camper van with camping gear, booked a spot at a private campground, monitored the weather – because it can get dangerous pretty quick – and off we went. We piled on a few extra layers, made a campfire under the stars and I loved every freezing minute of it. Christmas morning, Santa even found us, and left stockings stuffed with goodies. Mom swore off camping, but that's when it became an obsession for me. The mountains call my name, and I must go."

"If we're competing – you win." Shauna laughed.

"I'm not trying to compete. I was just going

with the woods theme," Gabe tried to convince her.

If you were a bystander observing Shauna and Gabe as they engaged in conversation, the easiness of manner about them was that of a delightful couple, not strangers.

On occasion, Shauna could hear the mountains calling out to her in Atlanta. She answered the call from time to time, day-hiking the Appalachian Trail with friends and her old boyfriend, drinking in the incredible wonder-filled nature walks like a wilted plant thirsty for life-sustaining water. As soon as she would park her trusty little red Jeep and step into the lush thick woods, she left her city stress behind and refreshed her mind with the amazing scenery of waterfalls cascading over the smooth round rocks accented with soft green moss, misty morning fog that hung low over the mountains like smoke resting high on the trees, and breathtaking vistas of layers and layers of mountaintops where you could see God's splendor for miles.

She kept to her day-hiking trips, but secretly admired those who took the adventure of a lifetime and trekked the 2,190 miles of the Appalachian Trail, or the AT as they would call it. She left that up to the rugged hard-core adventurers.

Eager to let Gabe in on her thoughts of mountain camping, Shauna veered from the Christmas talk. "I have to admit, on occasion I could hear the mountains calling when I lived in

Atlanta. I could do day-hikes, but I'm not a snake and bear kind of girl." Shauna then wagged her finger at him, anticipating his response. "And before you can say that snakes and bears shy away from humans, I decided that if you had to hide your food in a smell-proof, bear-proof bag and hang it high in a tree, so bears wouldn't come rummaging around the campsite for their dinner" – she continued getting a little animated with her hand gestures – "or you have to zip up tightly so you wouldn't wake up with a reptile that slithered in like a thief in the night, snuggling in the bottom of your sleeping bag – I pass on camping." She added, "I hope you're not offended."

He wasn't offended. He imagined her scrambling to escape the slithering sleeping companion from a mummy sleeping bag, collapsing the tent in the process. Laughter escaped his thoughts.

Ada's two-minute warning saved him from revealing his flight of imagination. Still smiling, Gabe suggested, "How about skipping to a one-word-answer question and we can save the rest for another time."

Sipping coffee, Shauna momentarily paused, perplexed by his laughter and the smile that still glistened in his eyes. She didn't know this man who sat across from her, and didn't have a clue if he was laughing at her, or with her. Insecurity crept in with self-defeating thoughts.

To escape her anxious, probably dubious, thoughts, she picked up the list, pretending to read it. She wanted a random pick, but it really wouldn't be random, since she had already read over the list. She suggested he pick the next question.

Unaware of her rising anxiety level, he casually suggested, "Okay, let's go with question... four."

That was the one question she didn't want to answer. Shauna thought it was a bit too personal and considered skipping to the next, but honesty prevailed.

Shauna read, "Question number four: What is the one word that describes the last year?" Shauna laid the list down, placed her hands under her chin, took a deep breath, exhaled, and said, "Challenging." She was guarded in her word choice. She wanted to be candid, deceitfulness was not her nature, but if honesty truly prevailed, she would have said, *traumatic*.

Without hesitation, Gabe replied, "Restoration." The scripture Ada read earlier, suddenly came to his mind. *You'll be known as those who can fix anything, restore old ruins, rebuild, and renovate, make the community livable again.* He privately questioned if that included his heart.

They both sat for a few moments in awkward silence, pondering hidden meanings.

Ada excitedly addressed the crowd, "Okay, it's time to choose your ornament of hope and get started on your special mission." Ada pointed toward Gabe and Shauna and asked them to lead off. They scooted their chairs back, led the way to the tree, and left the list of Christmas Conversation Starters for another day. Gabe wondered how many days.

Chatter filled the room as everyone eagerly fell in line.

As Shauna began, no one watching had any idea this beautiful and vibrant woman concealed her melancholy behind the mask of smiling depression.

Gabe watched in amusement as Shauna closed her eyes, used her hand as a blindfold, turned around two times as if she was playing Pin the Tail on the Donkey, groped around high in the tree, and randomly chose her ornament. A heart-shaped ornament.

Gabe noticed Shauna's puzzled frown when she saw the ornament she'd picked. More intentional than she had been, he moved his hand to his chin in a thinking pose. He studied the dangling trimmings methodically, and prayerfully selected a specific ornament. An angel; the messenger of hope.

Ada curiously watched them make their divine selections. With wishful thinking, her mind skipped from Christmas to designing a wedding cake.

Chapter Seven

Calm and considerate, Gabe sat back comfortably in his chair suggesting Shauna read her selection first. She unlaced the red ribbon that held the scroll with the request and began.

"There's this old man, Mr. Barnett, that sits on his porch and waves at my school bus every day. It doesn't matter if it's cold and rainy or snow on the ground, he's always there. Some of us wave back, but others make fun of him with funny faces or a hand sign with the middle finger that I would get a whoopin' for making. I think he's lonely, and from the tarp someone recently added to his roof, it looks like he needs help. He has an old shabby American flag flying on his porch. My mom says he's a veteran. I saw a story on the news about a veteran who died alone and there was no one to attend his funeral."

Thinking of her beloved veteran grandfather, Shauna's voice began to crack. She apologized, fanned her face with her hand, took a deep breath and continued. "The funeral home contacted a reporter, hoping they would feature it on the news and maybe someone would attend his funeral. Once the story was on the news, veterans came by the dozens to honor him at his funeral."

The little boy closed the letter with, "I don't know why we wait until someone dies to honor them. Why can't we help them while they're still living? I'm just an eight-year-old kid, without any money. I hope someone can help this man for Christmas. Thank you! Timmy Johnson."

Shauna didn't try to conceal the tears that flowed down her cheeks. She feared that in her state of mind, the floodgate would open and she wouldn't be able to close it. She reached for a napkin and dabbed her eyes. She noticed Gabe's eyes revealed he was more than the strong-and-silent type, as he fought against the urge to cry.

"Wow! That kid is wise beyond his years," he said.

Shauna added, "I think that's the most unselfish request I ever heard from a child." Adding some levity, she said, "And being Santa's little helper over the years, I've heard them all."

"Do you want to start planning on this request or read both of them first?" Gabe asked.

Hoping to give her space to recover, she suggested he read the next note. Gabe cleared his throat and began.

"I volunteer with a non-profit organization called, ACHIEVE. It is a ministry for single moms who are pursuing college degrees while raising children. ACHIEVE provides scholarships, financial assistance, and emotional and spiritual support to these low-income moms who are trying to improve their lives and the futures of their children. They are constantly battling the daily struggles they face in their attempt to escape poverty."

Gabe's heart ached as he kept his head down, reading the letter intently, trying to conceal his emotions. This story was his mother's story. She was once a poor single mom, who juggled parenting, a part-time job, and culinary classes to achieve her dream of a better life. It was an unrelenting struggle she conquered with the help of friends and strangers.

"This year, budget cuts eliminated our little annual Christmas party that we normally give for our moms and their children. We had to choose between food gift baskets or a party and small gift, so we chose what we felt the most practical – food baskets. My hope is somehow we can provide both. The kids always love the party with the special craft and treats. For some of the pre-school children it may be the only Christmas party they attend. If you could be our Christmas angel, you would bless the lives of twelve young women and their children. Phyllis Bowman, Volunteer."

Gabe reached for his coffee and swallowed a gulp, hoping to drown his emotions. Shauna reached over and dug through her coat pocket in search of another tissue. "OMG." Shauna dabbed her eyes again. "I'm glad I didn't load my lashes up with mascara, tonight. The scary crazy clown streaks would have been monumental!"

Gabe chuckled and was thankful for her comedic timing. Never could he imagine this amazingly beautiful woman being compared to a clown.

"I think we have our work cut out for us." Gabe rubbed the back of his neck, just like he did when he approached a daunting project. "I don't think we have enough time, tonight, to tackle the planning and brainstorming," he suggested. "How about we sleep on it, and get together tomorrow and brainstorm?"

"I like that idea," Shauna agreed. "I have a commitment in the morning, but I'll be free around noon."

"Let's take up where we left off tomorrow. I'll get here before the lunch rush starts. Send me a text with your order, and it will be waiting for you."

She hesitated for a moment to ask for his number, cognizant of her social media detox rules. She decided they were more of suggestions than a decree and could be lifted for these special Christmas-angel missions, and added Gabe to her contact list.

"I hate to rush off, but I just remembered I promised Mom I would lock up the henhouse before I left and I completely forgot." Shauna stood, tucking her phone in her purse, frustrated with herself that she broke a promise. "Mom would never forgive me if Dasher, Dancer, Prancer, Vixen, Comet, and Cupid were devoured by a racoon invasion." Shauna counted on her fingers, just to be sure not to leave out any chickens.

Intrigued and humored by the names, Gabe just had to ask, "You told me your mom was crazy about Christmas, but this is hilarious. Why only six chickens?"

"It's a small henhouse and she didn't want too many eggs she couldn't use. Otherwise, if anything ever happened to Rudolph, we could be on standby for Santa. Get this, she decorates the chicken coop with Christmas lights. You would think the chicks had their own Vegas show. Who does that?"

"I've met your mom and even worked with her on a committee with the town council. She's always been the go-to person for anything to do with the holidays, but I didn't know this extreme side of her existed."

"You don't know the half of it. I'm surprised she didn't glue little red Santa hats on them." She shook her head in bewilderment. "Got to go, see you tomorrow."

Bundling up, she turned and rushed out of the coffee house, leaving him staring after her in wonderment.

#

Shauna strapped on her seat belt and adjusted the heater to full blast to knock off the chill. Her high-neck puffer jacket took her mind straight back to Gabe. When he joined her at the table, he had laid his coat on top of hers, on the empty chair, and the fabric had absorbed his cologne. She inhaled deeply. His scent matched him. She thought he would be a perfect model for the REI outdoor sporting goods store. He smelled woodsy with a scent of a refreshing blending of cedar, sandalwood, and she detected a hint of musk. She could smell this all day long. She shook her head to clear away the scent and her thoughts. She didn't succeed. They lingered.

She pulled into the drive and noticed an inside light illuminating the family room in the cottage. She intentionally only left the bedroom light and outdoor porch lights on. She felt anxiety creep in as her heart raced. She consciously controlled her breathing to calm her nerves. Long, slow breaths in through her nose. Count to three. Exhale slowly through pursed lips. Repeat. She calmed.

Having been a victim of stalking, it became second nature to Shauna to survey her surroundings. At first it was cyberstalking, then it escalated to physical stalking. She was forced to change routines, carry pepper spray, and let her friends know her schedule – in the event of the worst case scenario. The move from Atlanta distanced her from her stalker, but the fear was always close at hand – but so was her pepper spray.

As Shauna stood in front of the door, reaching for the handle, the door flung open. Shauna stood face to face with her sister, Abby. Seeing the pepper-spray canister aimed straight at her face and Shauna's finger on the trigger, Abby yelled, "It's me!" and immediately dropped to her knees, hoping to escape the blinding effects of the spray.

Shauna saw Abby just before she applied pressure to the canister and instantly let go of it.

"What are you doing sneaking around this late at night?" Shauna demanded.

Abby was now sitting on the floor, resting back on her arms. "First off, I'm not sneaking around. I know the key code. I had Tyler drop me off and take home the kids, so you and I could spend some time together. And second, I could ask you why you're out this late at night."

Fear gave way to laughter as Shauna said, "You should have seen your face. I didn't know you could move so fast."

Abby realized she was probably in the wrong – this time. She joined in laughing. "What did you expect? My fight-or-flight response triggered into high gear to avoid temporary blindness. I just didn't take flight, I dropped like a rock to my knees." Sitting on her bottom, she reached out her hands for assistance. "The least you can do is give a girl a hand."

"I'll even do better than that. I'll make some hot cocoa and you can tell me more about Gabe." She pulled her sister to an upright position.

"Well, well, well. Little sis wants the scoop on the most available bachelor in town," Abby teased. "That I can do – but be prepared, it's more than a little sad."

Intrigued, Shauna drew her brows together at the comment. "How sad?"

Chapter Eight

Shauna managed to roll out of bed before the chickens had a chance to wake her up. She dressed layered, in all of her go-to activewear essentials for winter running, laced up her shoes, and found a scrunchie to pull her curls up into a floppy pineapple top knot. She grabbed her phone and pepper spray, and headed for the walking trail that picked up at the pond, behind the cottage, and lead you downtown to the train depot. It was a good morning. An outdoor run in the crisp, cold air always gave her a hormone surge for a major mood boost. She thought it gave the phrase "it's time to chill out" a whole new meaning. She plugged in her earbuds, opened the Bible app, scrolled to Psalms, tapped the audio button, cleared her mind, and began listening.

Her therapist had recommended Psalms as a prescription for depression. She said many of her patients found hope in seeking God and praying the Psalms. Shauna gave it a try and found it to be true, as the writer put words to her feelings and thoughts, when there were times she could not find her own voice – even to pray. She was glad she had chosen a Christian therapist who would recommend medication, if need be, and offered Christ-centered counseling.

Every so often she attended church in Atlanta with friends. It became more frequent when she experienced her dark times. It helped her move from darkness to light. Growing up, church on Sunday wasn't optional in the Murphy household, it was mandatory. But Gran was Shauna's walking Bible. She learned more from listening to her grandmother than any pastor in a pulpit. When she was younger and Gran would talk about the "Good Book," she imagined her Gran late at night, reading this mysterious giant book, filled with secret words to live by. As she grew older, she discovered Gran's pearls of wisdom were straight out the Bible. Gran had a way of teaching without preaching or judging. She was never an enforcer of the faith, but always an encourager of faith.

Before her foot hit the walking trail, Gran whispered in Shauna's mind: *Remember, child, joy comes in the morning.*

Shauna decided to run to town, listening; and run back, thinking. She politely waved at the Goose Whisperer, who was out bright and early feeding the fowl. She really wanted to stop and point her to the posted sign forbidding feeding, but she chose joy. Running at daybreak was not for the faint of heart, combine that with chilly temperatures and she almost had a private trail. Right before her train-depot destination, she unstrapped her iPhone armband to end the app, and she couldn't help but smile when the smooth audio voice read the Psalm: *Weeping may endure for the night, but joy comes in the morning.* Gran was at it again – quoting scripture without anyone noticing. She missed Gran.

Shauna did her best thinking while running. It was a perfect tool for brainstorming or problem solving. When she was assigned a new client, her award-winning ideas usually surfaced mid run. Today, her thoughts were not only on the Giving Tree project but on Gabe. She reminded herself she only had about twenty minutes left on her run and had to focus on one or the other. Gabe won.

The night before, Abby stayed until after midnight. Shauna always enjoyed girl talk, but listening to the story of the innkeepers at Spring Valley Inn was unexpected. Abby warned her it would be a sad story. It was more than sad; it was heart wrenching. In her time away from Spring Valley, and just popping in and out for quick visits, she hadn't realized that the Martins, the long-time owners of the inn, had passed away. She had a vague memory of their granddaughter who visited them in the summers and helped out at the inn, but they wouldn't be called friends. She felt a little guilty for not staying connected with the quirky characters that made her small town so unique. In preserving the historic inn, the Martins were heritage guardians of Spring Valley – her heritage. They had slipped away to eternity and she wasn't aware, or she didn't make herself aware.

Shauna was confident in her discernment. She enjoyed first-time meetings with clients, chatting casually about their business, focusing on the person and the plan. Never fail, she assuredly walked away with a game plan for their social media project, with a complete grasp of their branding, their goal, purpose, and direction for the entire process. She was bewildered by Gabe. His scars of grief didn't show. Did he wear a mask to conceal his sorrow? She was the master of masks. Surely, she thought, she would have picked up on that, or was she too self-absorbed with her own crisis to notice another's pain?

Her mind swirled with questions as she came running around the corner, stopping at the railroad crossing for a car to rumble across the tracks. Had he worked his way through the emotional stages of grief and landed on acceptance and hope? Had he experienced the same darkness of depression that clouded her days? She had so many questions, but didn't have the right to ask Gabe for answers. She had experienced grief with the loss of her grandparents, but couldn't image a young widower's journey.

The cold air bit into her lungs as she came to the end of the trail and pondered the most powerful question: How do you make peace with the God who gives and takes away?

#

Shauna made a pit stop to open the henhouse and feed the chickens. She was thankful that Abby must have closed the coop last night, before their little scary incident. That was the one thing her mom had asked her to do. Why was it so hard to remember to let them out in the morning, scatter feed, water, gather eggs, and lock them up at night? She always dreaded jury duty, but chicken duty topped it. She heard rambunctious coop chatter; hens anxious to make a run for it down the ramp. Shauna unlatched and opened the door for the brigade.

"Good morning, girls! You made it through another night."

As they cautiously made their entrance into the cold, crisp air, leaving the warmth of their cozy roost, she had to admit that she admired her mom's choice in chicken breeds. They were Plymouth Rock hens and she thought they were actually pretty with their black-and-white barring, with each feather ending in a dark tip. It was interesting how it resembled an old-cartoon jail uniform, but strikingly beautiful, in a chicken-kind-of-way. She smiled when the thought entered her mind that little red Santa hats would look really cute.

Their ear lobes and comb were red as was the face. Their beak horn-colored, and their beady reddish eyes always on alert. As one looked her straight in the eye and clucked, she repeated her grandmother's whisper to the chickens – "Joy comes in the morning!" As she filled the feeder with pellets and scattered some on the ground, they pecked, clucked, and murmured in contentment. She couldn't believe she was chatting with chickens.

The aroma of coffee escaping the kitchen and wafting in the air beckoned her to her parents' home. She peeked in the back-patio door before punching the key pad, just to make sure they were up. Her mom noticed and motioned her in the kitchen.

"You're out early for your run this morning." Shauna leaned down and they greeted each other with a kiss on the cheek. She almost smothered her mom with her shaggy pineapple curls.

Swiping the pineapple from her face, her mom asked, "Did you remember to feed the girls?"

"Yes, but just a minute, let me check the bottom of my shoes to make sure I didn't bring you any gifts from them." Chicken poop was the worst, so she decided to take off her shoes and leave them at the back door.

Her mom knew all about the gifts, she had special garden clogs for her morning ritual. She actually had time to feed the hens, but she'd hoped by asking Shauna it would give her daughter a reason to get out of bed before noon.

"Coffee smells great."

"Help yourself, your dad is still in bed. He should be up in a little bit."

Shauna poured herself a cup and sat down at the table with her mom.

"What do you have planned for the day?"

"Well, as a matter-of-fact, I volunteered for the Giving Tree project. After I take the kids to the train depot for pictures with Santa, I'm meeting with my teammate to brainstorm this afternoon."

She didn't mention the name of her teammate. Her mom didn't ask, because she already knew, and was pleased. Sometimes, she knew that if she pushed Shauna in one direction, she pushed back just as hard, and it led to nowhere. She hoped this would lead to somewhere, so she didn't push.

"Fantastic, honey. I was hoping you would find something Christmassy to do. Your grandmother always said, 'Act the way you wish you felt, and you'll start feeling the way you act.'"

"Yes, Mother Christmas, never fear, I'm going to be consumed with granting holiday wishes for the next three weeks." She reached over and teasingly pinched her mother's cheek. Shauna knew she meant well. Her mom misinterpreted her bah-humbug behavior. She wasn't moping, she was mending.

"If you have a few extra minutes would you do me a huuuuge favor and braid my hair?" Scrunching her floppy curls, she said, "I can only duplicate your braids in my hair dreams."

"Practice makes perfect, and I had a lot of practice with your locks, but I guarantee it will take more than a few minutes. We can do a loose

French waterfall braid, and use your scrunchie for the bottom tie."

"Great! I was hoping for a 'yes'." Like a magician pulling a rabbit out of a hat, Shauna pulled a wide-tooth detangling comb out of her pocket. "I came prepared!"

"Do you have a spritz bottle in there, too?" Colleen leaned over and tugged at her pocket. "Didn't think so, let me grab mine."

The spritzing began. Alice the cat curiously peeked her fury head around the corner to investigate the chatter that woke her from her slumber. She meandered in, performing a few yoga stretches any instructor would envy. She nudged and rubbed against Shauna's feet, purring and flicking her tail. Without an invitation, she jumped up and made herself at home in Shauna's lap.

With her comfort cat purring contentedly, Shauna sank her fingertips into her soft deep fur and mindlessly stroked her feline friend. As Colleen interlaced Shauna's hair, her caring touch kindled the childhood feelings of comfort and care. It felt like home.

"Ahh, this feels so good. The stress is melting away."

Brushing Shauna's hair, in an attempt to tame the tangles, was always a challenge, but it was Colleen's favorite time she spent with her little gingersnap. Images, from toddler to teen, flooded her mind. Mom braided and Shauna chatted. Between the frequent "ouch!" exclamations, she shared sweet moments with Shauna. Her baby girl didn't know that with each strand of hair, her mom whispered prayers. Prayers for safety, a mended heart, wisdom, character, health, strength, compassion, a heart for God, and dozens and dozens of other requests. She realized as she wove strands of hair, those moments wove their lives together. She hoped Shauna remembered and cherished that bond. *Lord, flood her heart and mind with peace.*

"The secret to a beautiful loose braid is adding in only a few strands at a time. It's messy, whimsical, and free, but somehow it all comes together beautifully." It was just like her daughter, she thought, whimsical and free. Her life was a little messy now, but Colleen had faith it would all come together.

She teased Shauna. "You know, if we could get a brush through your hair, with 100 strokes, you could see your future mate in the mirror."

Shauna had heard the enchanting folklore dozens of times. Her great-grandmother had sworn by it and passed the myth down from generation to generation. *If you had long, shoulder-length hair, a mirror and a hair brush, you could see a vision of your future mate. Just before sundown, sit in front of a mirror and begin brushing your hair slowly for 100 strokes. Then lean forward slightly and brush your hair down over your face. Peer through the veil of your hair into the mirror to catch a glimpse of your future groom.*

"As a teen, the only way I could get a comb or brush through my hair 100 times was with wet hair and a gallon of conditioner. I attempted several tries, with no luck. I didn't get a glimpse of my future groom, but I did have really soft hair." She softly patted her braids, inspecting her mother's handiwork. "Thanks, Mom, if it looks as great as it feels, I'm beautiful."

Colleen kissed her on the top of her head and agreed. "You're gorgeous! A little stinky from running, but gorgeous." She patted her shoulders. "Wrap that hair up carefully and shower."

"I can take a hint." She took one last sip of her coffee and slipped into her shoes. "I'll drop the kids back at the shop, after pictures with the big guy in the red suit."

"Didn't know I had extra help this morning. The sitter must still be sick." She placed her dishes in the dishwasher. "Oh, well, the more the merrier!"

Chapter Nine

I t was too quiet. Gabe walked into the empty kitchen for his mug of coffee. He missed the comforting sounds of the inn. The fire had silenced the footsteps, the muffled conversations behind closed doors, and the laughter that gave the inn life. And then, there was Robin. She still roamed the inn. He saw her everywhere. Not as a vision who silently strolled the halls at night, but the distinctly feminine imprint in her designs was etched throughout the building. He missed her scent. Jasmine and orange blossom, soft and subtle, and bursting with spring. She called it her English garden in a bottle. The fire stole her scent, too, it drifted away with the smoke.

He was grateful the Firefighters saved the building, but as the firetruck pulled away he realized the kitchen was a complete loss, and the rest of the inn had sustained extensive smoke and water damage. The restoration company assured him they would restore it like it never happened. They had to, the inn was Robin's dream and was all that remained of her. She had wanted to renovate the kitchen, but he had crunched the numbers and they decided to wait until the next year. He regretted that decision. Next year never came for Robin, and his penny-pinching left faulty wiring to ignite the fire.

His missed his small staff. They were like family and loyal to a fault. After the fire, when faced with unemployment at Christmas, they'd all agreed to consider these few weeks off for renovations as their paid vacation days for the upcoming year. He didn't want to lose them and they couldn't bear to leave Gabe in his time of need.

He reached for his handwritten list on the counter and checked another project off as complete. The painters had left the building! As soon as the commercial stove and new appliances arrived, the fireplace mantle was installed, and the final inspection complete, he could re-open. It surprised him that he was running ahead of schedule. That never happened. He'd considered opening for New Year's Eve, but after last night's Giving Tree reveal, he decided he needed every minute he could spare. He had been on the receiving end of kindness; now it was his turn to give, and he was up for the task.

Reminding him he wasn't entirely alone, Big Papi, his chocolate lab, picked up his empty dog bowl with his mouth and tossed it at Gabe's feet. A friendly reminder that dogs like breakfast, too. "Okay, buddy." Big Papi jumped on his hindlegs and rested his front paws on his human friend's waist, as Gabe rubbed his head. "You're a good boy.

Yes, you are, a good hungry boy." That was just enough approval for Big Papi to make a victory lap around the kitchen as Gabe filled his dog bowl.

Adopting Big Papi was one decision he would never regret. The funeral home had offered the presence of a therapy dog. Not familiar with the concept, Gabe asked his pastor to make the call – he had too many other decisions to make. Being a dog lover, it was an easy choice for the pastor. In his fog of grief, Gabe felt comfort when the dog would approach him at the funeral home, and lay quietly, curled at his feet. It was soothing. He'd closed the inn for a few weeks after the funeral. The deafening silence of the building haunted him. He decided, with a little prompting from his friends, that he needed his own therapy dog. At his investigative trip to the rescue shelter, Big Papi had him at his first hello-bark. His big old puppy-dog eyes sealed the deal.

The night Gabe brought Big Papi home, he put his paw on Gabe's leg, and buried his head in Gabe's lap, and that's when Gabe finally sobbed. It touched his heart; it's there, in his heart, that Big Papi made his new home. Gabe felt a little guilty renaming his dog and hoped it wouldn't confuse the pup. He came home with the sweet name of Cocoa, but the first night he gained the new name of Big Papi. Being a Boston Red Sox fan, David Ortiz – Big Papi – was Gabe's favorite player of all time. He'd helped Boston capture the World Series title after eighty-six years and broke the curse of bad luck in 2004, when he was the MVP of the American League Championship Series. Gabe's favorite quote of Ortiz's was, "It doesn't matter if we were down 3–0. You've just got to keep the faith. The game is not over until the last out." Every time he called out his name or petted Big Papi, the dog was a reminder to *keep the faith*.

Gabe's mind jumped to his lunch plans. "Big Papi, after we eat, I'll take you for a walk, check on our neighbors, then I've got to get ready for my lunch date." The dog didn't hear him over his smacking and crunching and Gabe didn't mind, at least he had someone to talk to. Gabe backtracked. "It's not really a date. Or is it? I guess you could call it a 'work' date." Gabe rattled on as he set the table. It became routine. Gabe set out one plate, one glass, knife, fork, and spoon.

He paused and stared at the place setting, almost frozen in time. The one place setting looked lonely, incomplete.

The dog inhaled his last morsel of breakfast and sat staring up at Gabe with a cocked head and a doggy perplexed look.

Gabe made a conscious decision. "Big Papi, I don't know if I'm ready to find love again, but it's worth a try."

Big Papi sensed his friend's mood had lifted and excitedly made one more lap around the kitchen, anxiously expecting his 'good boy' rub on his head.

Gabe wondered if Shauna was a dog person.

#

Her mom was right. The shower washed away the stink without turning her braids into a frizzy mess. Necessity is the mother of invention and Shauna discovered that the Turbie Twist hair towel she usually used to dry her wet hair, was just as effective keeping it dry, gently cradling her hairstyle choice for the day. Shauna was pleased with herself for rising before dawn. It was only 8 a.m. and, if need be, she was dressed to walk out the door, energized and ready to face the day. It felt good to have a purpose.

When she'd made the decision to file a sexual harassment lawsuit against her supervisor, whether she won or lost, she'd felt robbed of her career – her purpose. With the backing of their liability insurance to defend against lawsuits, human resources gave her a leave of absence with pay. They just considered it a cost of doing business. She considered it an attempt to buy time, and to isolate her with the hopes she would quit. She didn't give in to their intimidation, but she was in limbo for months. The attorney advised her to stay in Atlanta during the proceedings. She complied. But sitting alone in her apartment day after day was not good for her mental health. She wanted to work, but she knew if she tried to interview with another social media marketing company, she wouldn't even make it to a first interview. They would sabotage her online. She knew all too well the good, bad, and ugly of social media.

Shauna thought of how easy it was to stay connected through social media with her family and friends when she moved out on her own. It was her livelihood. It was the best tool for building a brand online and taking your product global. But it was dangerous. It made her an easy target for her stalker. When she'd tried to avoid her perpetrator boss, and pleaded with him to stop his sexual advances, he'd launched an online assault using social media as his ammunition. She couldn't run and hide and let this aggressor destroy her and her career. It had to stop.

They all knew that bad publicity posts on social media ruined careers and destroyed businesses. When her attorney convinced her company that they were not immune to social media disasters, the tables were turned. They'd agreed to a sizable settlement. Company officials also agreed to terminate the perpetrator and adopt comprehensive sexual harassment training programs. She'd won but lost so much.

Shauna decided it was time to move forward and not dwell on the past. She had signed up for The Giving Tree as a goodwill favor to Ada, and now after last night's reveal, she was determined to see it through and make at least two Christmas wishes come true. She had a couple of hours before she had to pick up the twins for their Santa pics, just enough time to start organizing the plan. She decided she needed some inspirational Christmas music to get her in the holiday mood. She found her phone, opened her Spotify app, and selected her dad's favorite album, *Appalachian Christmas*. He said it always took him back to his childhood Christmas when families gathered and their home was filled with music – with fiddling, bluegrass, and the mountain dulcimer. Her father was the musician in the family. She and Abby didn't seem to get that musical gene, but music was still a holiday tradition for the Murphy family. The one tradition she loved.

Shauna plopped down on the couch, nibbled on a breakfast bar, opened her laptop, and started a new social media content calendar file. She knew there were other ways to tackle the task, but this calendar was second nature for Shauna. She could plan ahead, batch her work, and note down all her brainstorming for later. Shauna loved hashtags, she wondered what could be their tag? They weren't crime fighters... Then she thought, "good deed duo." She added #gooddeedduo to her notes, along with #givingtree, #ornamentofhope, #veteransXmas and #achieveXmas.

She knew she had a tendency to push through a project without input from others. After all, she thought, she was the best of the best in her field. But today, she had a teammate. She hadn't forgotten Gabe, he seemed to be unforgettable.

Chapter Ten

Waiting until the last minute, Shauna broke away from her laptop, grabbed her coat, wrapped her scarf around her collar, and headed to the shop to pick up the twins.

Parking was always a challenge, especially this time of year, but she spotted a space close to the entrance of the parking lot and hurriedly began her track to the store. She walked past the Spring Valley Inn, wondering if Gabe was inside. She didn't see any contractors roaming around, so she thought he must be closer to finishing up the remodel. She wanted to drop in and poke her head in the front door to check it out, but she was already running late, plus she didn't want to appear too forward. Then again, she thought, I don't know how I want to appear.

Her breath in swirls of fog, Shauna picked up her pace, and maneuvered her way around busy shoppers strolling the sidewalk. She opened the door to the Olde Town Christmas Shop, stood for a moment soaking in the joy of Christmas, smiling at the familiar sight of wall-to-wall Christmas with ornaments, trims, trees, lights, and nativities. Even though she begrudged the 24/7 Christmas of her youth, she had to admit walking in the store was a festive wonderland. Since Abby had joined as assistant manager with her mom, Shauna wanted to explore, to look at every new idea that Abby had implemented, but she wanted to see the twins more.

She followed the chatter to the back of the room and caught a glimpse of them in the middle of a dozen kids working on a Christmas art project. Olde Town Christmas Shop was not just a retail store, her mom wanted to educate the next generation of folk-art crafters, keeping that connection to their heritage. Colleen hosted workshops throughout the year for beginners to advanced-level students, led by some of the most talented artisans in the area. Today they were making reindeer ornaments from small branches and evergreen clippings.

Before she could surprise the twins, Paige caught her eye and with a whoop she exclaimed, "Auntie Shauna! Come see my reindeer."

Passing her sister along the way, Shauna gave Abby a quick hug. "Oh my goodness, these are the cutest things I've ever seen." She reached and picked up one of the ornaments. "Did you make these all by yourself?"

"Well, everything was cut and ready for us, and the holes were drilled for the legs, but I'm putting it all together and look" – she pointed to its head – "I drew his cute little face."

Bryce chimed in from across the table, "See mine?"

"That's amazing, Bryce. Are you going to hang it on your tree, or give it to Auntie Shauna?" she teased him. Bryce sat silent for a moment, pondering the answer. Shauna chimed in, "I tell you what, you keep the reindeers you made today, and you can show me how to make them."

Bryce smiled in agreement, relieved he didn't have to part with his craft.

"Thanks for taking the twins to see Santa." Abby navigated her way around the little crafters, bumping a few chairs with her ample hips. "We're running a little late, so it will probably be twenty minutes, or so, before they're finished."

"So I'm not the only one that runs a little late?" Shana needled her sister who was forever pointing out that Shauna's clock was broken.

"Ha, ha. When you're working with a dozen kids, you'll have a good excuse."

"That's okay. I have some time. I just need to meet Gabe at noon. If I'm running late, I'll text and let him know."

"That sounds promising." Abby smiled and crossed her fingers.

"None of that, this is strictly for the Giving Tree brainstorming."

"Okay, little sis, if that's what you say." Abby winked at her.

Shauna strolled across the room to her favorite display, a private collection, that was always front and center. She ran her fingers over the life-size exhibit of the Corn Husk Christmas Angel. Shauna might have inherited her Gran's enchantment of angels, but not her artistic touch. A masterstroke of art brought life to a corn husk angel.

"It's stunning." A familiar voice interrupted her thoughts.

Shauna turned and Gabe and his dog stood behind her. She bent down to pet the dog.

"The sign said leashed pets are welcome, I hope that's okay." He was pleased she greeted Big Papi.

"Mom's okay with pets in the store. I know it will be tempting, but just don't let him pee on a tree."

"I was walking the dog and saw you through the window and I thought I would just get your lunch order in person." At least that's the excuse he came up with on the spur of the moment. He actually saw her through the window and did a double-take to make sure it was Shauna. The fairy-tale Rapunzel braid was enchanting. Somehow, with that waterfall braid cascading down her back, she had become the heroine of a fairy tale waiting to meet her prince.

He pointed toward the angel's red hair. "Were you the model?"

Teasing him she said, "Oh, you're really

good, Sherlock. You noticed the similarities."

"Who could help but notice?" Gabe smiled. He liked her playful ribbing. "I've read that this collection has been exhibited in the Smithsonian."

"You are correct, plus other museums and many of her pieces are in private folk-art collections." Shauna stood and admired the collection. "My gran was a prolific doll maker, but I have to confess, I wasn't the model."

"You could have fooled me, the face and detailing are yours, not to mention the red hair."

"Well, Gran always did call me her little Christmas angel, but I wasn't her inspiration."

"You've piqued my interest, what's the story?" Gabe focused attentively on her mystic blue eyes, as Shauna recounted her gran's story. Big Papi miraculously sat calmly beside Gabe and gazed up at the giant doll with a red bird perched on her hand.

"When my grandmother was a little girl, one winter she was walking back to her home from her grandmother's when a whiteout snowstorm hit. She lost her way in the woods and took shelter under a big evergreen tree. Hours passed as the sun faded, her family were out searching but couldn't find her. She said a little red cardinal flew beside her and sat on a little branch, singing and chirping, and kept her company under the tree.

Gran prayed out to God in her tears. She knew she would freeze to death if she didn't make

it home before dark, so she mustered up the courage to start walking, when a woman with beautiful red hair appeared on the path. The cardinal
that had kept her company flew and landed on
the stranger's outstretched hand. Gran had always
heard that 'when cardinals are near, angels appear'
and she said a blanket of peace calmed her as the
woman told her she would be safe and led her out
of the woods. On the edge of the clearing she heard
her parents yelling out her name and walked toward the sound. She turned to thank and hug the
woman, but she was gone." Shauna touched the
face of the corn husk angel. "That's the angel's face
and hair. That's why Gran called me her *little angel*."
A tear streamed down her cheek as she finished the
story.

"I didn't mean to make you cry," Gabe said
as he pulled a tissue out of his pocket and gave it to
Shauna.

"It wasn't you; I just miss Gran." She dabbed
her tears. "After Gran's experience, she started
making corn husk angel dolls and gave them away
to hurting, lost people, always sharing the story
of her Christmas angel. Hoping to give them a
message of hope and peace." Shauna stretched out
her arms motioning to the store. "That's what inspired this store."

"Who makes the angels now?"

"Mom continued the tradition, plus Gran
taught her craft to other artisans, but she was the
master. I think it's because of her real-life angel

inspiration."

Gabe couldn't help but stare into Shauna's lovely face, wondering if she was his Christmas angel.

The twins interrupted the moment and yelled out, "We're ready Auntie Shauna!" Then they noticed the dog and pandemonium pursued.

Gabe, afraid Big Papi's wagging tail would destroy the store, took control and led him out the front door. Shauna took lead as the kids followed closely, hoping to pet the dog. They stood for a moment outside the door allowing the kids to smother Big Papi with affection.

Shauna interrupted their fun. "It's time to go if you want to get pictures with Santa."

Bryce looked up with pleading eyes. "Can he come, too? We could have our picture made with the dog."

Paige chimed in, "We're not allowed a dog in our house because Dad is allergic. Pleassssse?"

Whether Gabe wanted to or not, Shauna suggested, "I'm sure Gabe doesn't have time today, you can visit with the dog another time."

Gabe shrugged and contradicted, "I've got time. He needs a longer walk and looks like he loves the kids."

The twins jumped up and down in excitement and Bryce asked, "Can we hold his leash? I promise we won't let him go."

"Sure, you guys can take the lead." Gabe handed the leash to Bryce and Paige.

"Y'all hold tight. There's a lot of people on the sidewalk. Don't overrun them," Shauna directed them.

Bryce stopped and looked up at Gabe. "What's his name?"

"Big Papi, but he'll answer to just about anything."

The kids led the way with Gabe and Shauna walking side by side.

"That's an unusual name for a dog," Shauna commented inquisitively.

"I'm a Boston Red Sox fan and Big Papi is my favorite player of all time."

"That's right, you're a Yankee."

Gabe laughed.

"What's so funny?" Shauna asked.

"I was just thinking about the first time I was called a Yankee when I was younger visiting my aunt in Asheville, North Carolina," Gabe reflected. "I grew up a Red Sox fan, Yankee was a dirty word in our household. So the first time someone called me a Yankee my mind went straight to baseball not the Civil War, but I was being jokingly discriminated against for my Northern-ness."

"I'm not a big baseball fan, but I do know who the Yankees are. But I've got to admit, my mind would first go to the Civil War not baseball." Shauna silently wondered what other cultural differences they held. "Was it hard to adjust when you moved here?"

"It took a while to adjust. Southerners live a slower paced life than I was used to, so I've learned to be more patient." Gabe gave the question more thought and said "Merry Christmas" to a stranger they passed on the sidewalk. "That's another thing I learned. It's okay to look people in the eye and say hello on the street. That never happens up north."

"I've not been much of a traveler outside of the southern states, except for vacationing in Hawaii, and they are welcoming with the Aloha spirit. I moved to Atlanta after college, so I've really only experienced southern living."

Shauna turned and smiled as Gabe continued.

"One thing that drives me crazy is no one uses turning signals. I've named it the 'Tennessee Turn' – you've got to be alert at all times."

Shauna laughed. "That's not true, I use my blinkers."

"You must be the only one in the county," Gabe teased her. "Plus, when the snow falls, all the drivers on the road act like they've lost all their driving skills. I grew up plowing through a foot of snow, I'm skilled. Tennessee drivers are clueless."

"I'm guilty!" Shauna raised her hand. "I have to admit, I hate driving in the snow. I don't like the feeling of losing control." *If he only knew*.

Walking side by side their shoulders brushed. Shauna nonchalantly stepped further away to avoid any more physical contact. It was a challenge. But she was determined not to allow herself to be swept up in emotions with a man she barely knew. She had to be careful – her mental state was still fragile.

They arrived at Santa's Train Depot and, as expected, it was crowded with excited kids and parents, many of whom she knew. The twins secured a space in line. Playing with Big Papi would help entertain them for quite some time. Gabe kept a close eye on the three, Big Papi wasn't around kids that often, but he seemed to be in doggy heaven with all the attention he received. The lick on her face grossed Paige out but Bryce loved it as they giggled and Big Papi's tail wagged excitedly.

Gabe and Shauna both greeted people they knew, but Gabe felt there was too much awkward silence as they stood in line. Every time their eyes met it was different than before. Searching the depth of her eyes he saw sympathy. He knew she knew. He wanted her to treat him the same as she had the night before. It was like night and day. He didn't want sympathy for the widower. He knew he would have to broach the subject first. He had to tell her his story with Robin, if he wanted a *their* story. Soon, but not now.

Finally, it was their turn for pics with Santa. As Shauna situated the kids and Big Papi with Santa, she leaned in and said, "Santa, I know your secret."

The man in the red suit winked at her and

whispered, "I just hope it's not in my immediate future," then let out a big, "Ho! Ho! Ho!"

Shauna joined Gabe as the elves finished prep for the picture adding a big red bow to Big Papi's collar. It brought out the dapper side of the pooch as he held his head high.

Gabe leaned in and asked Shauna, "What did you whisper to Santa?"

"Can't tell, it's a big secret."

"Is it the Santa coffin secret?"

Gabe knowing, surprised Shauna. She shot him a disappointed glance. "Well, I guess it's not that big of a secret if you already know."

"I saw it one day when I dropped in to your dad's workshop unannounced. Rest assured, I'm good at keeping secrets." He zipped his mouth closed.

Gabe gave Big Papi the sit command and right on cue he sat and gave a big slobbery smile for the camera. The kids were thrilled.

Shauna told Gabe, "I hope Abby won't mind that a surprise dog will be in their picture this year. I think I will sell it as an unexpected Christmas miracle." She laughed. "It would definitely be a miracle if the kids were gifted a dog. This would be the next best thing – a borrowed dog, similar to grandkids you enjoy for the day, but give back to the parents."

Gabe looked amused and offered, "He's available for doggy visitations any time."

"Don't tell them, they'll camp out at your

inn."

She gathered up the kids to take back to the shop and pried the leash from Bryce's hand to give back to its rightful owner. Gabe asked for her lunch order and headed back to the inn. As he walked away Shana thought that Gabe couldn't be all that bad since kids and dogs loved him. Plus, he'd promised to keep Santa's little secret. Maybe she would share her secret with him, someday.

Chapter Eleven

Armed with her laptop and the calendar she had already organized; Shauna opened the door to the Mockingbird Coffee House. The welcome Christmassy aromas of cinnamon, cloves, and spiced coffee combined with the familiar soundtrack in the background of the sweet sound of the Appalachian dulcimer playing carols was heavenly.

The night before, Ada had overheard Gabe and Shauna's conversation planning a lunch date for brainstorming and reserved a table in the back corner of the balcony.

"Merry Christmas, Shauna!" Ada waved from behind the counter. "Gabe is waiting for you upstairs in the balcony." Ada had a little gleam in her eye as she watched Shauna bounce up the stairs. Ada sent up a quick prayer, *Lord, bless them*.

"Merry Christmas, Ada. Thank you!"

Shauna saw Gabe unloading the tray. "I hope you haven't been waiting long. Sorry, it took more time than I allotted to get the kids settled back with Abby. It's true, twins are double the trouble."

She let out an exhausting whew.

Gabe looked up and smiled. "No problem. Your timing is perfect."

Shauna unbuttoned her coat and realized Ada had reserved the booth she had observed a couple snuggled up in a few days earlier, sipping their hot cocoa and seemingly deep in love. The scene had conjured up loneliness and loss, but today she didn't feel lonely.

"I'm starving. The breakfast cookie I nibbled on this morning has worn off. Ooh, that grilled pimento cheese sandwich looks amazing." Shauna scooted in the booth and eyed Ada's butter pound cake, thinking she might have to try it first.

"That's another Southern thing I've yet to try," said Gabe, pointing to her sandwich.

"It's incredible. I don't think I could live without pimento cheese. It's always in the fridge in our house. You'll have to try a bite." Shauna cut a slice and offered it across the table to Gabe.

Gabe put his hand up in disapproval. "I don't know, I'm not a fan of mayonnaise and it looks like mayo is involved."

Shauna was persistent. "I won't lie to you. There's mayo, but it doesn't taste like mayo, it's just creamy and cheesy. You'll love it. If you don't, spit it out. I won't be offended."

He couldn't turn her down. Even before it touched his lips, he scrunched his face like he just tasted a sour lemon. He took a bite from her fork. His eyes brightened. He conceded. "Surprisingly, it's good! I'll try a full sandwich the next time. Are you always this generous and pushy with your food or just with Northerners?"

"Stick with me and I'll have you eating cheesy grits for breakfast."

Stick with me, stuck in his thoughts. "You're a mind reader, how did you know I haven't tried grits?"

"It's definitely a south of the Mason-Dixon line dish and one that is an acquired taste. Northerners try them at *Cracker Barrel* and don't usually walk away fans, but there's more than one way to fix grits and they are delicious." She thought his reaction to Southern dishes was amusing.

"I'll make a deal with you. I'll try the grits if you try clam chowder." Gabe reached his hand across the table to shake in agreement.

Just thinking about that gooey, thick, fishy soup made Shauna grimace in a painful expression, pinching her lips tight together. Knowing it was hard to find clam chowder in a local restaurant, she called his bluff and shook his hand. "I'm game, if you're game."

Gabe smiled, cognizant that she wasn't yet aware of his culinary skills.

For the first time in a long time Shauna felt her appetite return and took a big bite of her sandwich. She popped open her computer and asked Gabe, "Are you ready to plan?"

"Let's get this show on the road." Gabe had his pen and paper ready. He decided he would wait

until after planning to discuss his marital status –
widower.

#

Shauna turned her laptop at an angle so Gabe
could see from across the table.

He suggested, "I have an idea, why don't you
sit on this side of the booth and we can both see
your files."

Before she could agree or disagree, Gabe
started rearranging her plate and coffee cup to join
his side. Shauna shifted in the booth and thought
maybe it was a good idea after all. This way she
wouldn't be staring in his intensely inquisitive
eyes.

Settled, now shoulder to shoulder to Gabe,
she unveiled her calendar of events.

"This is a short time to pull off these projects, but if we stay on task, I'm confident we can
get it accomplished."

Gabe laughed. "Are you sure you weren't
in the military? You sound like a drill sergeant."
From her reaction he realized the comment may
have come off a little rude. His Northern bluntness often did. Being kinder and gentler was his
continual work in progress.

"You saw the calendar and I'm sure you can
count," Shauna said, pointing to the computer
screen. "Counting today, we only have eighteen" –
she re-emphasized – "*eighteen* days to grant these
wishes." She stopped and looked him straight in
the eye. "Do you have a better plan?"

Gabe loved that he'd ruffled her feathers but he responded in a kinder, gentler way. "Well, you did an amazing job, I think everything looks great, but I do have an idea." He took a sip of coffee to let her even imagine that someone might have a better idea. "How about we contact Mr. Barnett and see exactly what his needs may be? I've only lived here a few short years, but the one thing I've observed is that people are very private and might be insulted if we just barge in to save them."

She hated to give in to him, to anybody, but admitted, "You're right about that. But what's your plan?"

"Ada provided us with all the contact information for Mr. Barnett. I could give him a call and see if we could meet this afternoon."

"Just call him up out of the blue and ask him to meet two strangers. That's your plan?"

Gingerly, he continued. "I think I'll use a little more finesse than what you've implied, but yes. A phone call today. A short visit today. That's not asking too much."

"I have nothing on my schedule. Go ahead and make the call." Shauna was confident this plan would boomerang right back in Gabe's face.

"Okay, listen and learn." Gabe reached for his phone and entered the number. "Mr. Barnett, my name is Gabe Anderson, I own the Spring Valley Inn. Ada from the Mockingbird Coffee House gave me your name... Yes, I love Ada too... I haven't tried it yet, but I hear the Hummingbird

cake is one of her specialties… The reason I'm calling is we're trying to grant a Christmas wish for
this boy named Timmy Johnson. I understand that
you may know him as the little boy who always
waves to you from the bus… Yes, he does seem
like a really sweet kid. We are trying to grant a
Christmas wish for him and thought maybe you
could help… Well, you may have more influence
than you think." Before he could refuse, Gabe continued. "Can I drop by this afternoon and discuss
Timmy with you? I'll bring you a slice of Ada's
Hummingbird Cake… Okay, see you in about an
hour."

Shauna's eyes were wide open in shock. "I
can't believe you bribed him with cake. Plus, you
were this close to lying." She held up her pinched
fingers together. "You're a smooth talker, but we
may get booted off his property. I'm wearing my
puffer coat for extra cushioning."

#

The drive down the curvy road was only a few
miles out of town, but the landscape changed to
rolling hills with a few cows snacking on winter hay stacked high in the hay feeder, with
thick woods in the background on one side and a
white-water rushing river on the opposite. Rick-
ety old houses, newer small brick homes, and
mobile homes dotted the countryside. Remnants
of flowering bushes and garden lilies that a few
months earlier filled yards were replaced with
Christmas lights, yard ornaments, and melting

snowmen, evidence of children playing on a recent snow day.

Mr. Barnett's house was tucked in a hollow at the foothills of the mountain just a few yards off the road. He sat on his porch, just as Timmy described, all bundled up in his worn Carhartt coat, as he watched the world go by. His eyes brightened when he saw Shauna get out of the car. He stood to extend a hand to welcome these strangers.

"Young man, you didn't tell me you were bringing this pretty little lady with you."

Shauna may have left her hometown for the big city but she'd kept her small-town Southern charm. It was part of who she was. "Hello, Mr. Barnett, I'm Shauna, and this guy needed someone to make sure this cake didn't fall in the floorboard on the way over." She handed him the pink cake box.

"Good Lord, little miss, I thought he was only bringing me a slice, not the whole cake!" He grinned from ear to ear. "This will last me all week." He winked at Shauna. "Or, maybe a day or two."

She noticed the whittling wood shavings beside his porch chair. Images of her as a young child visiting her grandparents deep in a hollow of the Appalachian Mountains raced into her mind. Her home had always been in the city limits of her little town, but her grandparents preferred the solitude and songbirds of the mountains. Her grandfather spent countless hours whittling on the front porch, carving the songbirds that called the mountains home. She was mesmerized by how he could take a tree branch and transform it into a realistic-looking bird that seemed like it could fly away from the twig at any moment. He always said he and God had something in common and quoted the psalm of the Lord saying, *I know every bird in the mountains.* Her grandmother was always sweeping wood shavings off of the porch. His legacy of wood carving songbirds fills the branches of their Christmas tree each year. Another memory of home and heart that brought her comfort.

"Come on in, it's too cold to stand on the porch." Mr. Barnett led the way as Gabe held the door.

Shauna went straight to the fireplace mantle. "I saw the wood shavings on your porch. I thought I might find some carvings in your home." She smiled as she admired his handiwork of little people, birds, chickens, and an array of forest creatures. "I come from a long line of whittlers and these are exquisite."

Mr. Barnett enjoyed the adoration of his carvings and chuckled. "I've been carving all my life. My grandpappy gave me this here pocket knife when I was about six or seven years old." He pulled the small knife out of his pocket.

Gabe noticed Mr. Barnett's lungs rattled when he laughed. The air smelled of stale cigarettes and dampness, but his lighthearted personality brightened up the delightfully dingy old house.

Shauna picked up one of the carved birds, tracing her finger over the intricate lines. "My daddy's most prized possession is the pocket knife his papaw gave him. He even opted to miss a flight when he forgot to leave it at the house once, and TSA wanted to confiscate his treasure."

Gabe listened as the two spoke in their Southern dialect. His grandfather from New England was too debonair for "Grandpa," he preferred to be called "Grandfather."

"I don't fly, but if I did, I would have done the same thing." He held it tightly in his hand. "They'll be prying this out of my hands when I leave this earth." He put his knife back in the safety of his pocket.

Shauna's mind wandered for a moment to her daddy's secret project, contemplating what type of custom coffin Mr. Barnett would request. He was unique and his life mattered. She imagined his whimsical carvings on the lid. She didn't share her drifting thoughts, but if she had, she knew he wouldn't have minded. Talking about faith, family, and the land is as natural as talking about the weather in Appalachia. Most mountain folk talk freely of the next life. Heaven. The Promised Land. Raised in the church, they are people of faith and believe their Creator is actively involved in His creation and has an eternal resting place prepared. Pre-arrangement of the type of funeral service and casket you want is a common occurrence. She thought he might even be tickled.

"Would you like a cup of coffee or tea? I'll put a pot on the stove."

Gabe answered, "Thank you, but we just had coffee at the Mockingbird. We don't want to take up too much of your time."

Mr. Barnett gestured to the couch. "I've got all the time in the world. Take your coat off and sit a spell. I don't get too many visitors. I enjoy the company." He sat comfortably in what appeared to be his favorite piece of furniture – a rocking chair; old, creaky and full of memories. He rested his elbows on the arm rest, wove his long tobacco-stained fingers together and rocked back and forth. "So, tell me about this special Christmas wish for my little waving friend."

Gabe proceeded delicately. "The little boy, his name is Timmy Johnson. He sits in the front row on the school bus and recently noticed the blue tarp on your roof and thought you might need a little help with fixing your shingles, so his Christmas wish was to mend your roof."

The sway of his rocking chair came to a stop. Shauna thought this visit would definitely be cut short, but she kept smiling.

Mr. Barnett protested, "Well, that was mighty nice of that little feller, but I don't need no charity."

Gabe didn't point it out, but the water stain on the ceiling and the randomly placed buckets on the floor disagreed. Gabe kept talking. "Timmy liked your flag flying on the porch and his mom said she thought you were a veteran. He was proud and impressed because he wants to join the army when he grows up."

Shauna was dazzled by Gabe's gabbing. She changed her mind about him being the strong, silent type. The more he talked the closer they were to Mr. Barnett saying yes.

Shauna added softly, "Mr. Barnett, don't think of it as a gift for you, think of it as a gift for Timmy."

"His note even made me tear up." Gabe pulled the wish-note from his pocket and handed it to Mr. Barnett to read. Shauna had no idea that was in the game plan. She was impressed.

Mr. Barnett's reading glasses sat ready on the side table. He put them on to decipher Timmy's wish. They automatically slid down his nose to rest on a comfortable spot. They sat in silence as he read.

In anticipation, Shauna reached over and grasped Gabe's hand. He glanced down at their hands and was pleased. When he lifted his head, their eyes met. Her eyes danced with high hopes that Mr. Barnet would agree. Or, he wondered, were they dancing from their touch?

The stalled rocker released and began moving back and forth. Mr. Barnett cleared his throat to push back the emotion that erupted in his heart. He was of the mind that grown men don't cry, especially in front of strangers.

"I guess, if this is what Timmy wants for Christmas, I'll go along with it. But don't be making a big fuss over me," he insisted. "It will be nice to meet him."

"That's great!" Gabe clapped his hands, thrilled with the agreement. "Would this Saturday be a good day for you, Mr. Barnett?"

Shauna gave Gabe a questioning side glance, fearful that wasn't allowing enough time to recruit volunteers. He smiled at her and gave a slight nod of assurance.

"I reckon that will be as good a time as any. Hopefully, the weather will work with us." He reached over the side of his chair to pick up a well-worn Farmer's Almanac to check its prediction.

Shauna pulled her iPhone out of her pocket to check the weekend forecast before he had time to flip the pages to December. "Looks like we're going to have a cold but mild Saturday. The temperature dips below freezing and some flurries in the afternoon, but we should have it wrapped up by then."

"Yep, that's here what the book says. But look out, sometime in the next couple of weeks, it's predicting heavy snowfall." He nodded his head in agreement. "All my life I've been trusting this little book to predict the weather, tell me when there's going to be a full moon in the sky, when to plant my garden, heck, it will tell you when it's the best day to fish." He laughed. "It's made my life a whole lot easier and never treated me wrong."

He didn't seem to mind but Shauna felt a little awkward having whipped out her phone so quickly.

"I bet my Almanac is more accurate than that fancy phone of yours. Your gizmo is like bringing a knife to a gunfight," said Mr. Barnett.

She laughed when he teased her, but found it odd that her weather app's extended forecast only predicted snow flurries for the next two weeks. Hopefully, technology would win this fight.

Gabe was clueless and lost in the Farmer's Almanac conversation, so he just faked it and joined in the laughter.

Shauna wished technology had never treated her wrong.

"What do I need to do to get ready for you?" Mr. Barnett had warmed up to the idea and started counting down the days.

Gabe assured him, "You don't need to lift a finger, Mr. Barnett. We'll take care of everything."

As Gabe and Shauna stood to leave, she took one more look at the wood carvings. "Do you ever sell your carvings?" His work was pure Appalachian Americana.

"No, I just whittle. Some people pass the time watching TV, I just whittle and give them away to family and friends as little gifts. I got boxes of them out in the storage shed." He pointed with his thumb to the backyard.

Playing curator and knowing he could generate additional income; Shauna planted an idea. "You should dig those out of storage and share your talent with the rest of the world." Sincere flattery always charmed. "My mother owns the Old Towne Christmas Shop and features work of local artists. I'm sure she would love to carry these in her store. That is, if you're interested." She didn't want to press him for an answer. "Just something to think about."

"I'll give it a ponder." He grinned. "Little lady, I might take you up on your offer."

Mr. Barnett shook Gabe's hand and gave Shauna a little pat on her shoulder as they left.

"I reckon I'll be seeing you two on Saturday." He added, as he always did, "Come back when you can stay longer."

#

Gabe started the engine, Shauna rolled down the window and waved one last time at Mr. Barnett waving back from the porch. He was endearing. He seemed a little lonely, but he'd just made two new friends.

"You were amazing. Who says Northerners are too blunt?" Shauna looked at him in wonderment.

"I think we made a good team. You opened up with your conversational Southern charm and I dealt with the facts." He added, "Timmy's letter was the closer. It really touched Mr. Barnett's heart."

As they drove the winding road home, Shauna started planning. "Saturday?" She raised her eyebrows and the pitch of her voice as she questioned his timetable.

"Hey, let me remind you that you just said, only a couple of hours ago, that we only have eighteen days. And if I remember correctly, you strongly repeated *eighteen days*." He grinned as his eyes strayed from the highway to hers. "We just accomplished the most difficult task of getting him to agree. The rest will be easy."

She reached for her phone and asked Siri to start a note. "Hey Siri, create a note called Timmy's Wish."

Siri replied, "OK, I created a note, Timmy's Wish."

"Really? You're inviting Siri to join our conversation." He gave her the disapproval under-the-brow look.

On any other day, she would have stayed the course and finished the quickest, most efficient note taking with Siri, today, she gave in. "I'll create it manually, but I'm using my phone, not a pen and paper."

He watched as she tapped the side of her phone as if tapping a pen in deep thought. He thought she might as well dig a pen out of her backpack and put it to good use.

"We know the roof needs to be repaired. He didn't have any Christmas decorations. How about bringing in a small tree and have Timmy decorate it with a patriot theme?" In lightning speed her thumps pecked the screen.

"That's a great idea. He's too young to be up on a roof, that will give him a project and will brighten Mr. Barnett's day."

"I can get the guys at the workshop to laser cut stars and heart ornaments from wood scraps and schedule a time for a craft table at the store and ask Timmy and any of his friends or family stop in and paint the ornaments. Mom will donate lights for the tree. Oh, and one of Mom's friends works at a craft store, and I'm sure she would ask for a donation of red, white, and blue ribbons and maybe some of those tiny flags for the tree." Refreshments entered her mind. "I'll get Abby to pick up a huge tray of Christmas cookies and hot cocoa packets and hot cups."

She made him laugh. "Whoa, you're on warp speed."

"Sorry, when I brainstorm, it's more like a tornado."

"We'll need some muscle for the roofing. I know a veteran that is involved with the local American Legion. I'll contact him to see if we can get some volunteers to repair the roof. I'm sure they will provide a new flag for his porch." Gabe turned his thoughts toward roofing supplies. "I'll also call the company who repaired the inn's roof after the fire. The owner goes to the church I attend. I'm sure he will be willing to help out. It's a worthy cause."

Out of curiosity Shauna stopped typing to ask, "You go to church?"

"Do you find that surprising?"

"I didn't mean it that way." She was flustered trying to dig out of the deep hole she'd dug herself in. "I meant to say, where do you go to church? It just came out wrong."

"Before I answer that question, I have one for you." They had most of the planning complete, he'd decided to broach the widower topic.

Shauna wasn't sure she liked the direction of this conversation. "Ask away."

"Prior to last night, did you know that I'm a widower?"

She took a shallow breath and softly sighed. "No. Abby was at the house last night when I got home, and told me your story." She didn't know what else to say. "I'm sorry for your loss." As soon as the words came out of her mouth, she wished they hadn't. It sounded clichéd.

He decided to be honest with her. "This morning when I saw you at the angel display at your mom's store, when you turned and looked at me, I could see it in your eyes. I knew you knew."

"See what in my eyes?"

"Pity."

Controlled, but with disappointment and anger she responded, "You misinterpreted. There was no pity in my eyes. Compassion. Sympathy. But not pity." The word *pity* triggered her anxiety. She endured the looks of pity in Atlanta when

her co-workers felt sorry for her and "the circumstance." She didn't want pity and she didn't give
pity. She wanted to run, but was trapped in a moving vehicle. She could feel tension gripping her
chest, suffocating her lungs. She took in a deep
breath, exhaled, and stared straight ahead at the
road.

If Gabe wanted more than friendship, he
knew he would have to tell her about his marriage, Robin's death, and his journey back to living,
but this was not how he'd envisioned the conversation. Immediately, he knew his mistake. Why
did he have to destroy a delightfully perfect afternoon? His *pity* response was too blunt. Earlier that
morning he felt she'd treated him differently, but
as the day went on it had felt as if there was no
past, just the present.

"I'm sorry, Shauna." He reached across the
seat in a loving gesture to touch her arm.

She recoiled.

Gabe quieted his voice. "I'm sorry. That was
the blunt Northerner in me speaking. I'm sorry I
misinterpreted your compassion."

He didn't know if he should just shut up or
keep talking. He quit.

The silence drove him insane. He continued. "You don't have to respond, but I want you
to know how deeply sorry I am. For the past three
years I've experienced every emotion you can imagine. Denial, grief, fear, anger, depression, doubt.
Most people don't know how to react to death.

Their eyes speak too often with pity. I hated that look. They don't know what to say. I didn't until I experienced it first-hand." He shared his inner thoughts. "I remember reading a quote from C.S. Lewis, in his book about his wife's death. If I remember correctly, I think it was called *A Grief Observed*. He said, 'No one ever told me that grief felt so like fear.' He was right, fear consumed me. The first few weeks and months you're smothered with attention, then life goes on. They live their normal life. Your life is imbalanced. You stumble through day after day. You wake, fearing what the next day holds. Life as you knew it, vanished into thin air. You're living but walking around lifeless. The loss is overwhelming."

She felt her heart soften. She realized they had both overreacted.

They had more in common than he knew. She too had experienced denial, grief, fear, anger, depression, and doubt. She had experienced loss. But there was a colossal distinction – she hadn't lost the love of her life. This man was sharing the most traumatic event in his life and she'd recoiled. She was ashamed. She knew she was guilty of letting her stressful past get in the way of her future. She knew she was better than this.

"I'm sorry, I overacted." She turned to look at him and reached across the seat to touch his hand.

His heart stirred with her sweet gesture. A feeling of peace washed over him and arranged his jumbled thoughts.

"I think I've grown closer to the Lord. In my suffering I had to decide if I was going to let it turn me bitter or let it draw me closer to God. That's why I love these mountains so much. In my darkest days, they were my refuge. My sanctuary. It's where I met God in my grief. I chose God. It gave me clarity. It's made me more compassionate to wounded people. That's when I became more involved in church."

He desperately wanted to pull the car over and park, so he could turn and give her his full attention. But he was afraid if he pulled over, she might make a run for it.

"I call my grieving and suffering days, my thunderstorm. In my thunderstorm, I finally let go of fear and found hope." He didn't know what wounds her heart held, but he felt he may have added salt to an open wound. "I would never hurt you intentionally, I couldn't cope with being responsible for turning your beautiful smile into sorrow."

Shauna liked being called beautiful, but wasn't ready to reveal her thunderstorm. She knew she had to say something, anything.

"My Gran used to quote: 'The Lord is close to the brokenhearted and saves those who are crushed in spirit.'" She left her hand on his. "It appears that He saved you. I can't imagine losing my spouse. Just when your lives began together, you were torn apart. I'm sure she knew she was the luckiest woman in the world to have been your wife." Shauna smiled, but inside she felt she may have revealed her inner thoughts.

"Thank you. That means a lot." He felt a short reply was best as he pulled into the parking lot at the Mockingbird hoping they would finish planning the event together. The air was heavy and he didn't know if she wanted to run to her car or stay and plan.

"Do you want to sit in the car and plan a little more?" He held his breath.

"Sure." She smiled that beautiful smile. "We'll make a to-do list. Then divide and conquer."

Hoping his luck would last, he took a chance and asked, "There's a Carol and Cocoa Sing-Along at Tulip Tree Music Room this Friday night at 7 p.m., would you like to join me? Afterwards, if we have any last-minute details we need to address, we can finalize them at the inn."

The seconds it took her to reply seemed like eternity to him.

"I'm free Friday night. I'll meet you there. It's a date."

Chapter Twelve

S hauna awoke to something unexpected – hope. She lay snuggled in the bed, with the cat warming her feet. She smiled. Maybe this was the beginnings of her new path. Gabe had found hope in his thunderstorm, maybe she'd found it, too.

She thought of how strange but how welcome it felt. She realized she had settled in the land of hopelessness for way too long. Somehow, hopelessness became "home" – comfortable, swallowing her up like an old comfy couch, where you struggled to get up so gave up and decided to just stay. Her family worried about her now, but if they had seen her a few months ago, they would have noticed a measured improvement. The dark days were behind her, she had to get control of her stress. Her anxiety. Her fears. The hope she sensed in her spirit was helping chase them away. She had this overwhelming urge to jump up and open all the blinds that she had kept closed to intrusive eyes. As she went from window to window, she decided she had lived in a dark cave long enough and was starting to see light.

Her Gran whispered in Shauna's mind, *The Lord is your light and salvation – whom shall you fear?*

Shauna answered out loud, "I hear you Gran!" and whispered a prayer, "Lord, light my path and fill me with courage and peace."

As she opened the blinds on the deck doors, a songbird cardinal, eating a sunflower-seed breakfast at the birdfeeder, greeted her good morning with a "whit-chew, whit-chew" and "purty, purty" whistle. She was surprised the movement of the blinds hadn't scared the pretty red bird away. He actually looked into her eyes as he sang. As if he had been waiting her arrival. Then she remembered the mountain saying, "When cardinals appear, angels are near." Perfect, she thought, I need a Christmas angel.

#

The long-tailed songbird stuck around and led her along the jogging path. It flew and bounced along in the air from one fence post to another, waiting for Shauna to catch up. She thought maybe her brilliant-red companion was her guardian angel for the day. Her routine to run and listen to Psalms proved to be great therapy. The verse that caught her attention today reminded her of Gabe's conversation. Psalm 9:18, *But God will never forget the needy; the hope of the afflicted will never perish.* She was so glad she allowed herself to volunteer for the Giving Tree. It was definitely turning out to be a boost to her Christmas spirit.

Finishing her run, before she entered her yard, she could hear the chickens cackling, demanding to be let out of their coop. She had hoped for happy chickens this morning, they sounded like angry birds. She picked up her pace to get to the coop and allow the chickens their fun and freedom.

Shauna thought of how her mother's backyard had literally gone to the birds. So far, Old Man Winter had only visited Tennessee and not set up housekeeping, however, the severe temperatures up north drove the birds south. Her mother kept the birdfeeders full for her famished feathered friends. Along with cardinals, on any given day you could spy black-capped Carolina chickadee, little gray peachy tufted titmouse with an echoing voice, yellow and red house finch, and even an occasional red-bellied woodpecker picking at tree bark. Not to mention crazy chickens, wild wandering geese and daffy ducks.

Her gran always told her that we needed to learn from our little birdy friends. Her words drifted in her mind. She could picture herself helping Gran fill up a birdfeeder as she passed along life lessons from the Good Book. *I like helping the good Lord by feeding the birds. But, they don't worry about tomorrow, they just fly to and fro, because they know the good Lord will provide, just as he provides for us. So, my angel, don't worry your pretty little head, the Lord will supply all your needs. You're always sheltered under his wings.*

Shauna had decided she needed a better attitude for chicken duty and the night before had searched the internet for a guaranteed solution for gleeful chickens. To her surprise, in order to enjoy fresh eggs in the big city, she learned that Jennifer Garner and Lady Gaga had joined the urban chicken craze and were raising chickens in their back yards. Since Shauna was now tending chickens in exchange for her lodging, she decided if the two celebrities could raise chickens, it couldn't be that hard. She could surely *wing it*. She made herself laugh. She laughed with chickens – that was a sign that today was going to be a good day.

#

Since returning home for the holidays, her new morning ritual included dropping in on her parents for a morning cup of coffee. Today, the house was empty, and so was the coffee pot. Her parents were already at work. So, Shauna opted for a latte and pastry at the Mockingbird

On her drive in, she realized that it was the first time in months her stomach wasn't screaming at her in discomfort, nor did she feel the need to pop a precautionary antacid. It seemed managing her emotional stress truly played a positive role in her physical well-being. She smiled thinking that was another thing her therapist was right about. Sometimes she questioned her advice, but today she was a true believer.

"Good morning!"

"Good morning, Ada!" She double-greeted her with, "Merry Christmas!"

"You're out and about early this morning." Ada grinned as she got a head start on Shauna's usual latte order – gingerbread. She couldn't help but notice the extra spring in Shauna's step and contentment on her face. She actually glowed. Ada recognized it as happiness. She shot up a prayer, *Thank you, Lord.*

"After my run this morning and completing chicken duty, my neighbors were out earlier than usual and left me alone to fend for myself. So here I am, fending." Shauna rubbed her hands together in anticipation as she eyed the pastries in the display.

Ada happily watched as Shauna contemplated her selection. She had known her almost her whole life. She remembered her first day of school, when Shauna was six years old, bravely entering the classroom, a bubbling, lively, and spirited student. Her red curls bounced when she walked and her blue eyes sparkled. She had always been petite, but when she returned from Atlanta she was skinny. Stress skinny. It was the opposite for Ada. When she was stressed out her husband could count on finding her in the kitchen, scarfing down food. Being a baker didn't help, her waistline was proof. She knew from chatting with Shauna's parents that her stress and anxiety this past year was off the charts and she had completely lost her appetite. Today, it appeared she found it.

"Let's go with a slice of your signature Hummingbird Cake. I know it's early for dessert, but at least it is chuck-full of bananas." She smiled and added, "They are the perfect fruit, you know, or at least that's what I'm told. I helped brand an organic fruit market and that was part of their marketing."

Ada pulled the cake out of the display and sliced a piece. "Speaking of marketing, if you have a couple of minutes this morning, would you chat with me a little about how to market with social media?"

"Absolutely!" She looked at the clock on the wall and was pleasantly surprised that she wasn't running late. She had a few extra minutes to spare before heading to help her mom at the ArtFull ornament workshop. She was more than willing to spend that time with her friend and confidant.

"You go on and find a table. Enjoy your latte and dessert breakfast and I'll be right out." Ada hurriedly took the orders of the next few customers in line, turned the order-taking over to an employee and went to the kitchen to grab her notes.

Shauna gobbled down every morsel of her cake. She sent an email to her daddy to ask if he could have his guys laser-cut three dozen stars and hearts from scrap pieces for the patriotic tree for Mr. Barnett. She knew what the answer would be, but she thought she would make it formal and email anyway. She also added that she needed extra time on the secret coffin marketing campaign, since she was slammed with the Giving Trees projects. She promised she would begin in January. Since Gabe had scheduled Mr. Barnett's project for this Saturday, several days earlier than she'd had in mind, she concentrated on planning one project at a time. First thing Sunday, she would start on the ACHIEVE project.

Shauna shot out a quick email to Abby, asking to schedule time for Timmy and friends to decorate ornaments. Just as she finished, Ada scooted in the booth, anxious to hear Shauna's professional thoughts. She was just as anxious to hear about the possibility of Gabe and Shauna being a couple, but would save that conversation for a later date.

"You know me, girl, I'm old school. A couple of the teens on staff opened a Facebook business page and said I needed to create, let me see" – she looked down at her notes – "a Twitter account, and something called Snapchat." She let out a sigh. "I'm too old for this online stuff, I'm willing to pay for your expertise, can you help?"

As Ada talked, Shauna had pulled up the Mockingbird's Facebook page. It wasn't awful, but it was close to awful.

She looked Ada straight in her eyes. "Before we go any further, I will not accept a penny from you, understood?" Thanks to the settlement, money didn't concern Shauna, plus she knew Ada couldn't afford her rates.

Ada would rather give than receive, but she accepted Shauna's gracious offer. If God dropped one of the best marketers in social media in the South on her doorstep, who was she to refuse the good Lord's benevolent blessing? Ada firmly believed in *Godincidences*.

"You're off to a good start by creating a Facebook page. It's the easiest way to reach people who love the Mockingbird. It definitely needs to be tweaked." She chose not to use the word that came to her mind – awful. She decided a softer, gentler approach was best for Ada. "If you keep your Facebook page updated, it can turn your audience into fans and fans into loyal clientele. When you drive customers to action, you'll increase business, and build a unifying coffee-house community." Shauna knew Ada wanted the coffee house to be a gathering place of blessings and free of any racial divides.

"So, you're saying there's hope."

"There's always hope." Shauna surprised herself with that phrase. A few weeks ago, those words refused to cross her lips. "If I can get you to do a little homework, by the first of the year, I can have your social media marketing up and running. I guarantee it will boost your sales."

"So, this is your revenge on your first-grade teacher who gave you too much homework."

Shauna chuckled. "The thought never crossed my mind." It felt good to laugh, sincerely.

Her mask of smiling depression seemed to be fading. "But take good notes." She pointed at Ada like a stern nun at a Catholic school. "I don't want to hurt your feelings, but I also want you to be thinking about a better logo design."

Ada's shoulders slumped. "I knew that was going to be on the top of your list. Graphic design is so expensive, I settled for an amateur when I opened the coffee house. That's one marketing decision I regret."

Shauna assured her, "Don't worry, I do graphic design, too, that's not a problem. I have something in mind, already. An engaging graphic sets the creative direction for your entire social media presence, so we'll have to knock that out first."

Ada looked at her with a blank stare. "You lost me at creative direction."

"You're fine. Just try to answer a few of these questions, and I'll take care of the rest."

Shauna rattled on about defining goals, defining customers, how to interact and engage, search engines, outsourcing online order taking, third-party integrations, and other unfamiliar terms.

Their roles had swapped, Ada was now the student.

#

'Tis the Season' are joyful words for the owner of the Olde Town Christmas Shop and other small business on Main Street in Spring Valley. The best days for the Christmas shop's holiday sales were Black Friday and the week that followed, and this year was no exception. Shauna had no desire to be in the family business, but from time to time would contribute her marketing skills. She was responsible for the shop's killer website and e-commerce set-up. Cyber Monday became their biggest e-shopping day of the year.

Shauna opened the door to a festive shop crowded with Christmas customers in search of the perfect ornament, delightful sales associates, workshop attendees, and little elves hard at work in the back, shipping out tidings of good cheer in merchandise, guaranteed to arrive for Christmas – just like Santa's workshop. Her mom orchestrated the team like a principal conductor of the Philharmonic, with her competent associate conductor, Abby, assisting, waiting for her big break.

Abby loved working in the Christmas shop with her mom. They were two peas in a Christmas pod. She was perfect for organizing and recruiting local artisans to demonstrate their work and conduct workshops, passing along their Appalachian folk-art legacy. She was responsible for adding the personal holiday decorating service for homes and corporations, and had plans to expand and open the Comet Cookie Company, a reindeer themed cocoa and cookie shop, complete with a cozy fireplace and comfortable seating for watching romantic Christmas movies.

As Shauna stood in awe of what her family

had created, she changed her mind about her crazy Christmas mother. Christ was the center and driving force of her mother's heart, home, and business, and it was reflected in her shop.

As Shauna passed her gram's corn husk angel display, she could hear her whisper, *Christmas brings hope.*

#

Shauna was knee-deep helping Abby with the Art-Full tree ornament workshop when a couple leaving the store caught her attention. The woman held their keepsake ornaments tucked safely in their shopping bags. Shauna noticed the man open the door, and gently touch his companion's back. She thought of Gabe. She knew he was falling for her. His gentle touches on her shoulder, her hands, her arm, the way he cupped the middle of her back as he held the door, guiding her through the threshold. They were all signals that showed he cared. He wanted to protect her. He wanted to comfort her. She knew she was falling for him too.

Chapter Thirteen

G abe sat on the welcome bench outside the music room, patiently waiting for Shauna. As she saw him from a distance, she noticed he didn't have his head buried in his phone, like the majority of people who sit alone, absorbed in their media bubble. He sat back comfortably on the bench, under the glow of holiday lights. People-watching. He smiled and greeted those who strolled past, enjoying the cozy little historic town, all draped in holiday cheer. She pulled her collar closer around her neck to protect her from the chill and hurried along. She hoped he hadn't sat out in the cold for too long.

She was at the crosswalk when he saw her. The first time they'd met, he felt his heart flutter – this time, it raced. He promptly stood and walked in her direction. He hadn't seen her for almost forty-eight hours, but it felt like days. When they locked eyes, they shared spontaneous smiles. When he was in arm's reach, he took her hand. She accepted his gesture, and felt a surge of joy. They walked together, side by side – the perfect pace, she thought.

"Hi!" Gabe grinned.

"Hi, yourself!" The breath puffs reminded her of the dropping temperature. "Are you freezing? How long have you been sitting on the bench?"

"Oh, just a few minutes," he fibbed, he'd wanted to make sure he was there when she arrived. "It's not that cold. Remember, I'm used to a foot of snow being on the ground by this time of year." Reluctantly, he unclasped her hand to open the door to the Tulip Tree Music Room.

The gentle touch on her back didn't go unnoticed. She beamed.

They were greeted by the owner, Tom, an aging hippie who in retirement found his folk family and kindred spirits in Spring Valley. He stood out in the crowd. He preferred longer hair pulled back in a ponytail and casual, often offbeat, clothing. Together with his patchy beard and rimless granny glasses, his appearance took you back to the 1960's. Back to where dulcimers had a bit of hippie history, where he was introduced to this intriguing instrument in the folk music movements, listening to the sounds of Peter, Paul, and Mary and the dulcimer goddess, Joni Mitchell. Dulcimers gained popularity during the counter-culture movement, but the "Mother of Folk" and mountain dulcimer player Jean Ritchie's roots were deep in Appalachia. So, when Tom and his wife stumbled on this folksy town, they fit right in. Eventually, he joined the Main Street merchants and opened the Tulip Tree Music Room where he sold handmade instruments, and offered private and group dulcimer classes. He was one of this folk-art town's treasures.

Tom never met a stranger and was just as laid-back and friendly as his appearance. "Welcome! And Merry Christmas!" He greeted Shauna and Gabe. He knew Gabe from the Spring Valley Inn and enjoyed stopping by to chat from time to time, filling Gabe in on all the town gossip. He and his wife, Barb, had settled in Spring Valley close to fifteen years ago, so, Shauna was also no stranger to Tom.

"I haven't seen you for..." He scratched his head trying to remember. "I don't know how long." He gave Shauna a big hug.

Gabe observed and thought how even after living in the South for five years, the friendly hugging tradition was still foreign to him. The first time he met Robin's grandmother, she was very charismatic, and hugged him so tight he thought he would lose his breath. When she let go, she took him by the shoulders to see if he was still breathing, because he had completely gone stiff and didn't hug her back. That started a joke in their family that, because he was from the North, he didn't know how to love. He disagreed but went along with the jest. For his family, hugging was reserved for close family relationships, not fringe friends and acquaintances. But after attending church in the South, he discovered that the

Christian sense of "love your neighbor" is more in-grained into the culture than it is in the North. He found himself slowly getting more comfortable with hugs and genuinely *loving your neighbor.*

Tom patted Gabe on the back and directed them to the refreshment table. "We're waiting on a few people, before we get started. Have a cup of cocoa and Christmas cookies while you wait." He pointed to the framed photos on the wall. "Shauna, check out the new portrait. It's fab! I think you'll be impressed." He gave her the thumps up.

As they stirred their cocoa, Shauna gave Gabe a tutorial on the store. "I can't play, my daddy is the musician in the family, but I always loved coming in here with him."

Gabe and Shauna meandered slowly to-gether around the room, as they admired the ar-tisan crafted instruments that lined the walls. "Since Daddy's world is wood, he taught me how each piece of wood makes slightly different tones." She touched a light-colored instrument. "This one is my favorite. It's made from the tulip polar tree, which gives it a genuine mountain sound."

Gabe nodded his head. "Hence the name of the store."

"Exactly!" She nudged his shoulder. "I bet you didn't know I was such an expert in all things."

He laughed. "I'm learning fast."

"What I love the most about this store is the history on the walls. This is Appalachian history at its best."

They both tilted their heads slightly to take in the gallery of vintage portraits of musical mountaineers, holding their prized instruments.

Shauna let out a little gasp when she saw it. "OMG! This is what Tom wanted me to see."

She knew why Tom was drawn to this portrait. The young girl had a bohemian appearance, yet her home was hidden deep in the hollow of the mountains, far away from the influence of the counterculture movement.

The portrait was a vintage sepia photo of a fair, plain, but beautiful young woman dressed in a simple, long-sleeved white cotton dress, her hair pulled back in a braid, loose wisps framing her delicate face. The soft sunrays poured light over her hair and touched the deep leaves of the laurel bush that served as a backdrop. With her head slightly bent down, and eyes in a forlorn gaze, she looked angelic. Her long, thin, leathery tanned right hand held a garden bonnet, used to shelter her from the sunrays. She leaned gently on a wooden fence, that appeared it might fall from too much pressure. Her left hand rest on an hourglass shaped mountain dulcimer, with carved out heart shapes, that allowed sound to project full through the sound holes. The image was an inspiration for folk music for generations to come.

"It's a Doris Ulmann portrait." She was in

awe. "This is incredible! He must have paid a fortune for this piece of history; it should probably be in a museum."

"I've seen her work, but I'm not that familiar," Gabe admitted.

Shauna was more than eager to fill him in. "She is noted for her Appalachian portraits. In the late 1920s she and folk musician and collector, John Jacob Niles traveled the mountains, valleys, and hollows documenting the people of the Appalachians."

Shauna's gaze remained on the portrait of the girl as she spoke.

"Some people loved her work; some people hated it. Those that hate her photography think she romanticized images of mountain people. She was a wealthy socialite from Park Avenue and traveled the backroads in a chauffeured driven Lincoln." She lifted her nose in a snobbish gesture. "As she turned her lens on Appalachia, she was known for selecting the poses and props, to fit the idea of what the rest of the world thought of Appalachia."

She pointed to another picture of a mountaineer with his fiddle. "Paul Buchanan was known as "The Picture Man." He called the mountains home, and captured images of Appalachia because he was just trying to make a living charging five and ten cents for a picture. He let folks pose and portray themselves as they wished to be remembered."

Gabe said, "So, what I'm hearing is, it's another the North verses the South kind of a thing."

"I didn't say that, but I do think it's ironic that a New Yorker's celebrated photographs would capture the soul of Appalachia."

Tom announced it was time to begin. They made their way to a couple of empty seats. As the soothing sounds of the dulcimers began, Shauna's thoughts were still on the portraits that surrounded them. These storyteller images watched over them. It was almost haunting. Their music still echoed down through history to the musicians playing carols in the room.

She thought of how, just a few days ago, she questioned if she should return to the mountains. Tonight, staring at the portraits, she felt she was discovering who she was – finding her roots. She left Spring Valley trying to escape 24/7 Christmas, but she also wanted something different. She wanted to escape the derogatory, stereotypical imagery of the region. Maybe what she was looking for was right in Spring Valley all along. Her heritage.

#

Unbeknownst to either Shauna or Gabe, they both thought their Christmas spirit was dead. The carols this evening was one more step to bringing it back to life. As they critiqued the sing-along with rave reviews, they strolled hand in hand down the moonlit, snow-dusted brick sidewalk that led to the inn.

"We've got a full winter moon tonight. Are you up for another cup of cocoa and a firepit?" His fingers slightly tightened on hers.

Shauna thought for a moment, then nodded. "If you add a log to the fire and provide blankets, I'm in." Silently, she was anxious to see the inn. She could only remember a handful of times she had been inside. But she could wait for a personal invitation.

They entered through the courtyard. Big Papi's keen ears were on alert. He barked.

In anticipation she would agree to the campfire, Gabe had the wood and tinder stacked and ready. He bent down and lit the fire.

"This is a great firepit. It's fancy, fancy." Shauna admired the courtyard and stood next to the fire. She wasn't crazy about the smell of burning wood, but tonight she wouldn't complain. She was under the stars with Gabe.

"We renovated the courtyard a few years ago for the weddings we host. A firepit was top of the list for cool fall and cold winter nights. Guests love it." He noticed Shauna wrap her arms around her chest in a self-hug. "I'll run in and retrieve a blanket. Do you mind if Big Papi joins us?"

"No, that's fine, I don't mind. Bring him on out." As he walked away she reminded him, "Don't forget the cocoa." Then added, "With extra marshmallows."

The moon cast a soft golden glow on the courtyard. From the layout she recognized it as a small version of an English garden. The thought came to mind that Gabe's wife would have been the designer behind the landscape, he didn't seem to be the English garden type of guy. He was more forestry, rustic and rugged. She admired the fairy-tale iron gate and stepping stones that led to the firepit and branched off to the simple, but elegant wedding gazebo. They were nice features for a story-book wedding. She could faintly hear the soothing sound of rippling water over rocks, from the babbling brook that ran through the back of the property, adding a nice touch to the ambiance. The cold had sent the perennials to hibernate, only remnants of the plants remained. She imagined that in spring a romantic meadow-like floral landscaped, filled with lush flowers, would burst with life. She tended to the fire for a distraction. She was annoyed with herself for thinking such romantic thoughts.

Big Papi interrupted her sentimental thinking as he dashed to greet her. Before he had a chance to knock her over into the firepit, she bent down to pat him. He loved it.

Gabe handed Shauna her cocoa, sat next to her on the bench and spread the blanket over their laps.

"Are you warm enough?"

"Yes, this is nice."

Their conversation turned to any last-minute details for their early-morning project for the Giving Tree at Mr. Barnett's home. To their surprise, everything was set. But Shauna had un-finished business. Her goal included more conver-sation with her host.

"The twins would love this campfire, but they would insist on smores."

Gabe volunteered, "The guests love smores, and roasting chestnuts! You can bring them any time. It's really fun when there's snow on the ground."

"Last night, the twins burned their Christ-mas list."

Gabe gave her a puzzled look. "Were they naughty and burned their list for punishment? I've got to say, that's pretty severe. Your sister is tough!"

Shauna laughed out loud. "Oh, my gosh, no, it's an old mountain tradition." She could hardly speak from giggling. "I'll give you some Christ-mas trivia." She dove deep into the details, like a local tour guide who led tours of this historic lit-tle town. "Children around the world began writ-ing letters to Santa in the later 1800s, but in the mountains of Appalachia, children would burn their letters in a fireplace and 'fairies' would carry their messages up the chimney and deliver them to Santa."

"Really? I've never heard that."

"That doesn't surprise me, you being from the North and all." She smiled as the reflection of the fire danced in her eyes.

Gabe sat straight up. "I've got an idea. We

have a fire. I'll grab paper and pen and let's burn our wishes. If we're lucky, the fairies out here hiding in the courtyard, will whisk our wishes off to Santa."

She playfully punched him on the arm. "You're making fun of me."

"No, seriously, I want to do this. It can be a new tradition." He silently hoped a new tradition with her. He jumped up to go inside for the paper. Gabe was surprised to see that Big Papi stayed content at Shauna's feet. His dog liked her, too.

They secretly wrote their lists. Gabe tried to peek, but Shauna covered hers up with her hand. They tossed them in the firepit. The papers quickly caught fire. They watched as their wishes of hope hitched a ride on the tiny flecks and floated up into the air.

"What did you wish for?" Gabe knew she wouldn't tell, but asked anyway.

"I'm not telling. If I tell, it may not come true. If you want to know, you'll have to find a little fairy hiding in the laurel bushes and bribe her to let you in on the wish."

Wanting to know more about her than just her wish, he changed the subject. "So, tell me about your job in Atlanta." He didn't want to think about her leaving but asked, "Are you returning right after Christmas or do you get to stay through New Year's?"

She held her mug to her lips and took a sip and thought how she really was enjoying the evening and didn't want to go down this path, just yet. But she knew she had to have this conversation sometime. She decided that maybe in the veil of darkness, it wouldn't be so intrusive.

"I'm not just home for the holidays."

That definitely piqued Gabe's interest. Would she be living in Spring Valley permanently? The next sentence deflated that thought.

"I left Atlanta for good, but I don't know where my next job will be."

She was not being very forthcoming, so Gabe gave her space, but wanted to know more. He opted for an easy question. "Will you stay in social media marketing?"

"Absolutely! I've had offers as far away as Seattle, but I'm weighing all my options."

"I've been to Seattle! I spent two weeks on vacation exploring the mountains of the Pacific Northwest on day-hikes. The scenery was breathtaking. I even glided down granite rock in a snow-melt flow. Now that was crazy."

"You love your mountains, don't you?"

"I don't think I could live life without them."

Shauna confided, "Sometimes I think about moving far away. Then, I think about starting my own agency. Lately, I've appreciated being close to family. All I need is high-speed internet, a computer and my phone. Spring Valley has all three."

Gabe liked that train of thought. He sipped his cocoa.

"I left Atlanta because I felt I had no other choice." She braced herself, ripped the bandage off her emotional wounds, and told him the whole ugly story.

Gabe refrained from interrupting and sharing what he thought of the perpetrator, her stalker. Jerk. Pervert. Bully. Lowlife. Snake. Instead he listened.

His heart had been shut tight for so long. Emotions opened the door. He wanted to protect her. Comfort her. He wanted to give her refuge in his arms.

She shivered. He didn't know if she was trying to shake off the past or the chill of the air. Gabe put his arms around her shoulder. Cold brought them close; close enough to kiss.

She hadn't been ready in body or mind for the gentleness of his kiss. He lingered and she savored each moment.

Gabe drew back briefly to look into her eyes. Her faintly closed eyelids slowly opened and locked on his.

A saying came to his mind: *redheads are sunshine mixed with hurricane* – a perfect analogy of the tempest in his heart, driven by this heavenly being. He was beginning to believe their chance meeting was a supernatural event.

If a shooting star shot across the sky, if snowflakes filled the air, Shauna was unmindful. There was only the contentment of this moment. Their lips met once again for a deeper kiss.

Gabe lifted his head and looked at her, though her eyes were bathed with contentment for a moment, they clouded over with fear. He knew that look; he had seen it in the reflection of his own eyes.

She nervously pulled away. For something to do, anything to do, she stood and started folding the blanket.

He didn't stop her. He patiently watched.

She wanted to run. She wanted to stay. Her emotions confused her.

"Thank you for the campfire cocoa. I think it's time I head home." As she walked through the iron gate, she turned and assured him, "The evening was lovely."

Gabe longed for this mystifying woman to stay in his arms, but knew he had to let her go.

"I'll see you tomorrow."

#

Gabe lingered around the firepit, stroking Big Papi's fur. His dog's love was unconditional. He always brought Gabe comfort. The last time he'd sat around a winter campfire in the courtyard was with Robin. Guilt abruptly smothered his feelings for Shauna, like the smoldering embers. The coldness of the winter night brought to mind when Gabe's heart was once so heavy, weighed down with never-ending grief and sadness. Unintentionally, he added extra layers of emotion. Abandonment. Fear. Guilt. Emotions piling one on top of the other, adding to the loss of Robin and the harshness of his personal winter. A heart too heavy to allow another entry. Months, then a year passed, then two. With faith and hope in the God who gave him strength, he slowly took off a layer, then another, and another. He weathered his winter. He recalled the promise that gave him strength, *The Lord is close to the brokenhearted; he rescues those whose spirts are crushed.*

Gabe reminded himself again and again that he survived. He had been rescued. He could live on. His heart was open to a new season of love. He felt such a strong connection with Shauna. Who was he kidding? Gabe's lovesick thoughts came face to face with his reality. He knew it was more than a connection, he was falling in love with her. But he felt he was adding on those heavy extra layers of emotion, again. This time fears. The fears he told Shauna he had conquered with the help of scripture. He felt so hypocritical. But the fear of forgetting Robin, the fear of rejection, the fear of the unknown, piled on. He asked himself, was his future in Spring Valley or did it only hold his past?

All that remained of the dying fire were sizzling red coals that flickered, hissed, and sparked – gasping for air. He reflected when not so long ago he gasped for air, but now he could breathe. Before surrendering to the warmth of the inn and sleep, he gazed one last time at the winter moon that rested above the mountains – the place where he met God in his grief. Corralling his thoughts, he heard the mountains calling, or – he questioned himself – was it a divine whisper? *Choose faith over fear. Live without fear.* Those words of action began spinning through his mind. Prompting him to choose.

#

Shauna lay in bed, thinking of Gabe. His soft penetrating gazes. Eyes that seemed to read and reach her soul. But she struggled. She felt she was competing with two ghosts. Robin and a ghost of herself. When she evoked her father's words, "You are courageous, you are strong," it brought back the fearless girl for a while, but doubt and fears would emerge and cause her to vanish into the ghost of herself.

In all reality, she knew Robin wasn't competition. Robin was an existence of Gabe's past. Did he look to the possibilities of the future? Not forgetting, but honoring, the past. Shauna had to do the same and become a woman of promise and a future. She wasn't a ghost. She was alive. She had to live. As her eyes surrendered to sleep, her gran whispered in her thoughts the psalm, *Sustain me, my God, according to your promise, and I will live; do not let my hopes be dashed.*

Chapter Fourteen

Saturday morning clocked in bright and early. When Gabe and Shauna arrived at Mr. Barnett's, roofing supplies were stacked neatly in place in his yard. As Gabe took inventory, momentarily he was distracted by the mountain backdrop, the perfect setting for this little property. There were times he thought about selling the inn and building a cabin in the mountains he loved. The mountains where he sought refuge from his grief when he lost Robin. The mountains where he found God. The quiet mountains where God whispered his name. He smiled and wondered if Shauna would live in a cabin in the woods.

Shauna carried in her tree-decorating supplies. Gabe wasn't aware that she stopped, stood at the window, and watched him lost in his thoughts. She wondered what occupied his mind. Was it her story she'd shared with him the night before? Or was it the kiss? As volunteers arrived, she continued to watch him interact with each new arrival. He was confident, friendly, and gracious to all who answered the call. There was something deep about this man. Something different. Something appealing.

Mr. Barnett sat on the porch waving, as each vehicle pulled in to help grant Timmy's Christmas wish for Mr. Barnett, their brother-in-arms. After handshakes, bear hugs, and friendly back-slaps were exchanged, at a little after nine, the buzzing noise of hand saws and the thwack of nail guns began filling the air. By noon, the roof was completely transformed, ready to withstand the winds, rain, and snow that lay ahead, for years to come. A new flag waved proudly in the breeze, decorative lights for the porch were hung, and promises made to return in the spring, to paint the interior ceilings. Watching this army of volunteers in action was nothing short of a miracle.

On his own, Timmy cut the little Christmas tree, tied it on his mother's car, and carried it into the house. Shauna, Timmy, and his mother leveled it in the tree stand and began decorating. Mr. Barnett was outside and Timmy wanted the tree completed before he came inside the house, so they worked quickly in tandem, as if they were professional tree decorators. When they stepped back to admire their creation, they were pleased at their patriotic masterpiece. Timmy grinned. It was beautiful and the perfect festive addition to Mr. Barnett's quaint little home. Timmy placed a wrapped gift under the tree.

Next to the tree was a little bookcase. On the top there were three books that lined the shelf like soldiers standing at attention. The yellow tattered covers beckoned Shauna to draw closer. She couldn't resist vintage books. They intrigued her, as she imagined those from ages past, who once turned the pages. When she picked up one of the books, the cover read: *War Department: Basic Field Manual – Soldier's Handbook – July 23, 1941.* When she read the date, she realized her papaw and Mr. Barnett had served their country in the same war. With recruits coming from such a small mountain area, chances were they had known each other. Papaw didn't speak much of his time in war, he locked those memories away somewhere deep in his soul. Maybe, she thought, she took after him, locking away haunting memories.

She remembered seeing a picture of a smiling young Papaw thousands of miles away from the family and mountains he loved, posed in the middle of a group of South Korean soldiers, capturing on film a stalled moment of war. Her grandmother told her that he taught English to his fellow Allied soldiers. She smiled, imagining Koreans learning and speaking Southern-fried English.

She knew Timmy would be interested and assumed Mr. Barnett wouldn't mind if they took a peek. Together they carefully flipped through the pages.

Timmy called for his mom to join them on the couch. "Mom, this is all about being a good soldier."

"If you're thinking about being a soldier, that might give you an idea of what to expect. What does it say?" she inquired. His mom didn't know if he would follow through with his childhood dream of one day joining the army. As a mother, she found it hard to think of such unsettling thoughts.

He began reading out loud. "One: Be obedient. Obedience means to obey promptly and cheerfully all orders of your commish..."

He stumbled on the word and Shauna sounded it out. "Commissioned and noncommissioned officers." She explained to Timmy that meant the people in charge.

His mom added, "I like that one – be obedient." She rubbed the top of his head, messing up his hair.

Timmy ran his hand through his hair as a makeshift comb and continued. "At first you cannot be expected to know the reason for everything you are ordered to do. As you remain longer in service and you understand more of the reasons for military training, you will find that everything has been figured out as the result of experiences in the past."

"Number two: Be loyal. Loyalty means that you must stand by your organization through thick and thin." He took a deep breath and kept reading intently, "Number three: Be determined. Determination means the bulldog stick-to-it-ive-ness to win at all cost... Determination to win means success in battle. Number four: Be alert. Always be on your guard. A good soldier may be pardoned for failure, but never for being sur-prised. And last, number five: Be a member of the team. Teamwork means that each man gives everything in his power to make for success of the whole unit. Unless you play your own special part the team may not win."

The three of them didn't notice that Gabe and Mr. Barnett had quietly entered the house and stood near the doorway, listening to Timmy read from the soldier's manual. Gabe admired Shauna as she assisted Timmy, she didn't appear to have a worry in the world. Her little new friend had no idea she carried the weight of the world on her shoulders.

Mr. Barnett walked over and took a seat in his rocking chair. "I see you're learning on how to be a good soldier, Timmy. That little book saved my life on the battlefield and taught me life les-sons to live by when I returned home."

Timmy only knew of make-believe war played in his video games. He nodded at Mr. Bar-nett, trying to imagine this frail old man in battle.

Shauna watched the two chat as strangers became friends, as one generation passed the baton to another. She raised her eyebrows as she reflected on the words Timmy read and thought the characteristics of a good soldier could not only build strong platoons, but the same principles would benefit families, businesses, and churches. The scripture verse, she learned in Sunday school long ago, came to her mind, *Endure hardship with us like a good soldier of Christ Jesus.*

Today, Mr. Barnett was remembered. His hardships were lightened by fellow soldiers.

Mr. Barnett turned his attention to the brightly lit patriotic tree and winked at Timmy through tear sparkling eyes. "Now that's the best and brightest Christmas tree I've ever seen." He noticed the ornaments were handmade. "Did you make these stars and hearts?"

"I didn't cut them out, but I decorated them." Timmy smiled from ear to ear.

"They make the tree shine. Maybe someday if your mom will bring you over, I'll teach you how to whittle." He took one of his creations in his hand and showed Timmy. "Would you like to learn how to whittle?"

Timmy wasn't really sure if he knew what whittling meant, but he knew that Mr. Barnett had handmade the little wooden bear he held in his hand. "I sure would!"

His mom smiled; she was proud of her son.

Shauna thought that if there ever was a man who bled red, white, and blue, it had to be Mr. Barnett. She had him and Timmy pose in front of the tree for a selfie for the Mockingbird Facebook page, then she and Gabe had everyone gather outside in front of the house for a group picture. Everyone agreed Timmy's wish was amazing and they were honored to be a part of making the wish come true.

Gabe prayed a silent prayer thanking God for today. It had been a blessing – a Christmas miracle, all because a compassionate little boy thought more of others than himself and hung an ornament of hope on the Giving Tree.

Chapter Fifteen

After the last vehicle left the property Gabe and Shauna waved Merry Christmas to Mr. Barnett.

Gabe pulled onto the highway then glanced at Shauna's face, which was beaming with pride in a job well done. "I don't think that could have gone any better, do you?" he said.

"It was incredible! Everyone gave 110 percent and went above and beyond what I ever would have expected." Shauna's eyes teared as she thought of the farewell scene. "Seeing Timmy hug and salute Mr. Barnett ripped my heart out."

"I admit, I fought back the tears. Timmy is an incredible young man. I hope he carries this gift of giving with him the rest of his life."

"Whoa!" Shauna grabbed the dash when the car hit a slick spot and started to drift. The temperature had dropped, making the roads a recipe for disaster.

"We're okay. I got it," Gabe assured her.

Just as Shauna thought, being only a few miles away from home, there shouldn't be any more problems, a truck came out of nowhere and crossed the center line. The raging river on the right side of the road left Gabe with nowhere to steer away from the impending collision.

It happened.

Gabe sat in the emergency waiting room anxiously expecting an update on Shauna's condition. He would have preferred to pace the hallway but the ER doctor insisted he be seated, since he had just been involved in an accident. He'd walked away from the accident with some scrapes and bruises, but Shauna was loaded into the ambulance unconscious with blood streaming down her face. He broke out in a sweat from the thoughts and fears that swirled around in his head. He needed a bottle of water. He made his way to the closest vending machine. He didn't have to ask for directions, he knew this place like the back of his hand. The same hospital where it seemed like only yesterday that he was allowed to pace the hallways, waiting and wondering about Robin's condition. The same hospital where he said his final goodbyes to Robin. The same hospital that couldn't save his wife. He prayed they wouldn't lose Shauna.

Swallowing the cool water forced Gabe to calm down, and for the first time since leaving the accident he began to breathe easy. Why hadn't they told him anything? He didn't know what he would do if Shauna didn't wake up. He played the scene over and over in his head. He couldn't swerve away from the truck into a freezing river. He hit the brakes, hoping to soften the impact. That's all he could do. But what if that wasn't enough? She'd looked fragile and pale, like a ragdoll. They let him ride in the ambulance. She didn't know, but he held her hand the whole way. Would he ever get another chance to hold her hand?

A gentle touch on his shoulder jolted him out of his frightening thoughts. Gabe looked up and saw Ryan and Colleen Murphy. He stood, not knowing what to say to Shauna's parents. Ryan seeing the pain and fear in Gabe's eyes reached and gave him a bear hug, patting his back with strong comfort pats.

"Everything will be okay, Gabe. It will be okay."

"The charge nurse in the ER knows Shauna. She called as soon as the ambulance arrived. We jumped in the car immediately." Colleen wasn't as calm as Ryan. "Have you heard anything?"

Biting his lip to push back the tears, and rubbing the nape of his neck, Gabe shook his head. "No, they haven't told me anything. It's driving me crazy."

"Well, somebody is going to tell me something." Colleen's determined-mother love was going to get an answer, one way or the other. She marched to the nurse's station. Not seeing the nurse who called, she asked the woman sitting at the computer. "I'm Colleen Murphy, my daughter,

THE ORNAMENT OF HOPE

Shauna, was brought in quite some time ago, and we haven't been updated on her condition."

The nurse pecked on her computer. "I'm sorry, I don't have any information. All I know is they are trying to stabilize her and I'll let you know anything as soon as I can."

Gabe heard the word "stabilize" – his heart sank.

That was not a satisfactory answer for Colleen. "Would you page Brittney, the charge nurse, please? She's a personal friend and I need to speak with her." Colleen didn't leave the station until she personally heard the nurse mumble in her lapel mic and ask Brittney to come to the front station.

"Mrs. Murphy?" Colleen turned and saw Brittney.

Brittney touched Colleen's arm and guided her back to Ryan and Gabe in the ER waiting room. Brittney was known for her compassionate bedside manners and dealing with anxious relatives.

"Let's have a seat. The doctor gave me permission to update you on Shauna, but Dr. Brook will be out shortly."

The motion of sitting gave them all a couple of seconds to calm.

"She's awake," Brittney said quietly. "She had a gash on her forehead, that's been stitched." Seeing the worry on Colleen's face, she said, "A plastic surgeon was in the building and the ER doctor asked him to stitch, so the scar will be barely visible."

Gabe and Colleen both let out a shaky breath and Colleen said, "That's good, but what else are you not telling us?"

"As I said, she's awake but she experienced a blow to the head and has a concussion—"

Colleen interrupted, "Did they do an MRI?"

"That's a good question, but no, and the reason is, images of a concussed brain may look normal as concussions generally don't show up on and MRI or CT scan. She has a headache, confusion, a little nausea and vomiting, and sleepiness."

The door opened to the waiting room as a doctor walked in. Brittney stood and introduced Dr. Brook to the three. Colleen was sure her daughter would be pleased with the physician, especially one who was considerate enough to allow a plastic surgeon to stich up her patient.

"Rest assured, Shauna is doing fine," said Dr. Brook. "I know Brittney filled you in on her condition. Since she experienced a blow to the head, I want to keep her overnight for observation. If all goes well, you can take her home in the morning."

"I would like to stay with her tonight. I'm assuming that's okay." Colleen's tone let them know it really wasn't a request.

"Absolutely, if you don't mind sleeping in a recliner. I'll have the attending nurse bring you a pillow and blanket."

Ryan asked, "Can we see her?'

Dr. Brook advised, "Since Colleen is staying,

I would ask that you just pop in and say hello. With her nausea and vomiting, she may not be up to a real visit."

Ryan turned to Gabe. "I'll go in and give her a kiss and let her know you've been here waiting, and see if she feels up to seeing you."

Gabe nodded in agreement. Brittney escorted Ryan and Colleen to Shauna's room.

Gabe sank in his chair and for the first time noticed the waiting room was filled with festive Christmas decorations and people. Worried people. Waiting for word – any word. How could he have missed them before? He smiled at a little toddler playing with his toy truck on the floor around the base of a Christmas tree – oblivious to worries and woes down the hallway. The tree gave him and the little boy a flicker of hope.

#

Shauna heard the sound of impact as the truck slammed into their car, crunching metal, Gabe's voice – then silence.

Her mind floated to consciousness as she heard her name faintly being called out.

"Shauna, can you wake up for me? Shauna? Shauna?"

The calling of her name slowly compelled her to open her eyes to a blurred face that gradually came in to focus. She didn't recognize the face but she seemed to be pleased that she was awake.

"Shauna, I'm Stacy, do you know where you

are?"

Shauna shifted her gaze to an IV catheter in her arm, tubing, and bag of fluid hanging from a pole. "I assume, I'm in a hospital." She had never been a patient in a hospital, but had visited them on many occasions. She had a whole new perspective from the view from her bed.

"Yes, you were in a car accident tonight. You have a concussion and a few stitches; the doctor wants to keep you over night." The nurse fiddled with the monitor. "How are you feeling?"

Before she could respond, Shauna motioned for what she recognized as a barf bag sitting on her tray. The nurse quickly managed to place it under Shauna's chin, just in time.

"Does that answer your question? I'm nauseous and have a craaazzy headache." Shauna was slow in speech.

The nurse smiled and wiped Shauna's mouth. "I'll be your nurse for the night. If you need anything, push this button." She showed her the hand control pendant connected to the hospital bed. "I'll turn off the lights, it should help with your queasiness. I'll keep the doctor informed to see if she wants to give you something for your nausea."

The fog in Shauna's brain lifted and the car crash flooded her mind. In a panic she asked, "How's Gabe? Was he hurt?"

The nurse assured her, "If you're referring to your companion, he's fine. They treated him in the

ER and released him."

"Is he here?"

"I can check for you. I'll step out just for a minute, if you think you're okay."

Shauna nodded as her pounding headache caused her to rub her forehead and discover the bandage. It's no wonder I have a headache, she thought, imagining what horrors lay beneath the covering.

Shauna saw familiar faces when Brittney opened the door with her parents in tow. She looked beyond them and didn't see Gabe.

"Oh, honey, are you alright? We were so worried." Colleen rushed over to her bedside and held Shauna's hand.

"I'm okay." Wanting to know about Gabe, she asked, "Is Gabe injured? How about the guy who hit us?"

Ryan joined his wife beside Shauna and gently stroked his daughter's hair above her bandage. "Gabe is fine. He's pretty shook up and worried sick about you, but he's fine. He's been in the waiting room this whole time." Her dad bent over and kissed her lightly on the forehead. "Your mom is going to stay with you tonight. You should be able to go home in the morning. The doctor suggested I just pop in for a minute. Do you want to see Gabe for a couple of seconds?"

Before he finished his sentence, Shauna grabbed the fresh barf bag the nurse had left, lifted her head off the pillow and hurled.

"No, I don't want him to see me like this. Just assure him I'm fine." She wiped her mouth, lay back on the bed and closed her eyes. *Please, God, let me be fine.*

Ryan left his baby girl and wife and found Gabe waiting just outside the door in the hallway. He told Gabe that Shauna wasn't up for visitors, but assured him she would have a full recovery. Ryan didn't know Gabe well, but he knew him well enough to know that Gabe cared for his daughter. Assuredly he advised, "Just give her some time, she's had a tough year."

Even though Gabe knew the story he appreciated the love and respect of her father for not divulging his daughter's secrets. They weren't his to tell. Gabe was exhausted and didn't want to share that he knew about Atlanta, thinking it would lead to a longer conversation. He did know that this accident would be adding insult to injury.

Ryan offered to give Gabe a ride home, since his vehicle was out of commission. He took him up on his offer.

Hospitals were meant for healing. They were also a place where life begins and life ends. As they walked to the parking lot Gabe was disappointed, but relieved. He exited through the doors. He glanced over his shoulder, looking at the third-floor center window of the room Robin succumbed to cancer, when he solemnly walked that same parking lot, broken and alone. Tonight, was a different story. Shauna was alive, safe in her room. He was bruised, not broken. He had hopes he and Shauna would be together.

#

The stalker entered her dreams.

Shauna's own gasp brought her out of a sound sleep.

"Shauna? What is it? Are you in pain?" Curled up in the recliner, her mother dropped the outdated magazine that was keeping her mind occupied, jumped up, and went to Shauna's side.

"I'm okay." Determined to erase the image from her mind, and to stop her shivering, she consciously controlled her breathing to calm her nerves. Long, slow breath in through her nose. Count to three. Exhale slowly through pursed lips. Repeat.

"If I learned nothing else from my therapist, the breathing technique she taught was worth the money." She continued to breathe herself calm. "I must have panicked when I woke up and realized I was in a hospital."

It was only a little white lie. She didn't want to worry her mother about her menacing dream. The stalker had reappeared, lurking outside her apartment. Tormenting her psyche with crippling doubt. Stealing her sense of security. Robbing her joy. She was safe now, every day she felt stronger. Her nightmares just had to catch up with reality. His haunting visits in her dreams were getting less frequent. She thought they had died away. Maybe the pain medicine and trauma of the accident brought them back to life.

"I've been right here all night." Colleen pat-ted her daughter's trembling hand. It wasn't the time to urge Shauna into sharing what else she may have learned from her therapist.

Shauna wanted to share her fears with her mother, but she couldn't. She was a grown woman, not a scared little girl who needed her mommy to scare away the monsters. However, Shauna thought it was sweet and comforting to know she was by her side during the night.

"Thank you for staying with me, Mom, I know how busy you are. You'll be a walking zom-bie at work."

"Don't worry about me, you worry about getting better." Colleen fluffed her pillow and pulled the blanket up to warm her daughter's shivering body. "Abby is taking care of the store today. She said she'll drop in to check on you after work."

"Speaking of the store. Where's my back-pack, I want to show you something."

"The policeman managed to grab personal belonging and sent them with Gabe in the am-bulance." She rummaged through the tiny closet. "Here it is, what do you want?"

"The man we visited yesterday is a whittler and to show his gratitude, he gave me and Timmy a cardinal ornament he whittled. I told him you may be interested in selling his work in your store."

Colleen preferred curating artwork for her business, but this wasn't the time to voice her thoughts. She found the bird secure in the bottom of the bag and was taken by surprise.

"This is masterful. It's almost identical to what your grandpaw would carve." Thinking of her father's prized pieces, her finger traced the delicately carved feathers of the little bird. "I would love to represent this artist."

"I thought you might. He says he has boxes of whimsical creatures in storage."

Colleen sat the red carving on her tray thinking, *When cardinals are near, angels appear*.

"It's a good thing he gave this to you before you left, I think your guardian angel worked over-time last night." Colleen whispered in gratitude, "Thank you, Jesus."

Shauna almost nodded off to sleep, but willed herself to stay awake by talking. "Did you get any rest?" she inquired.

"I got a few winks in. However, you slept soundly all night." Colleen smiled. "Correction, you slept loudly all night. You snore louder than your dad." She couldn't resist to add, "At one point, I thought it was the freight train passing in the night."

"I don't snore!" Shauna insisted.

"Hate to tell you darling daughter. Yes. You. Do."

"Give me a break. I'm on pain meds," Shauna grumblingly conceded. Rubbing her bandage on her forehead, she asked, "When do I get to go home?"

"The nurse was in earlier to check your vitals and said everything looks good. You managed not to throw up during the night. Dr. Brook should be in by eight this morning and, hopefully, will release you."

#

Gabe awoke with one thought on his mind. The woman that lay in the hospital bed was all that mattered. The final repairs on the inn, the Giving Tree program, they were just temporary projects and gifts. What he felt for Shauna was an enduring love, a divine gift. He stretched out his aching legs. He could never have imagined a month ago that he would have fallen in love with a total stranger at Christmas. He had hoped for the likelihood of love in his future, but not the possibility of it arriving so soon and unexpected.

Well, he thought, as he dragged a hand through his hair, he couldn't look away when he first saw her at the Mockingbird. He had finished his meal and was drinking the last drops of his coffee when he saw Abby and this outrageously beautiful woman walk in. He lingered long enough as they settled at their table. As he exited, he strategically walked by their table to say hello and get Abby to introduce him to her companion. Maybe he was already in love with her then. Love at first sight: was it possible? It was nothing new, scientists believe that love at first sight can be real, but staying in love is the deeper challenge. He was up for this challenge.

He wanted to be with Shauna, not just for this Christmas. But for next Christmas. Forever. For all of their future Christmases.

There was an emotional fence she'd built between them. The fortification for her fears. Her father had advised him to give her time. He would give her time, in hopes she would dismantle the fence. He felt he was good for her. He knew she was good for him.

Big Papi preferred the prohibited "under cover" sleeping, but had found a happy medium, curled up like a ball at the foot of the bed. He lifted his head and looked annoyingly at Gabe. He ignored the early-morning intrusion, whined a little, closed his eyes and went back to sleep. Gabe didn't have to eye the clock to know it was early. The sun still hid behind the earth, leisurely yielding to daybreak. The only scattered light in the room illuminated from the hallway light, he must have left it on when he fell into his bed last night, weak from exhaustion and worry. The clock on his nightstand read just past five. His muscles ached, but the few hours of sleep were enough for now. He opened the container of extra-strength Tylenol he had left last night on his nightstand, and popped two pills. He reconsidered and popped three. He was sure a hot shower would loosen the muscles and ease the pain.

His grimaced face escorted the moan when

he guardedly lifted his t-shirt over his head. The mirror affirmed his suspicions. The tenderness around his chest and black-and-blue patterned horizontal marks were remnants of the seat belt that saved his life during the collision. He'd managed to apply an ice wrap on his ribs before he went to bed. It had helped. The bruises would fade and heal in a few days, but he would never forgive himself if Shauna didn't recover quickly or, even worse, hold him responsible for her suffering.

Chapter Sixteen

For Shauna, the morning moved at a snail's pace. After the ride home from the hospital, her mom had made sure she had everything she needed. Giving in to her daughter's pleas, she reluctantly left Shauna alone to put a few hours in at the shop. She warned Shauna that she would call every two hours to make sure she didn't have any complications from the concussion. She even brought Alice to the guest cottage to be her cozy comfort cat, and insisted Shauna wear her comfy snowmen holiday pajamas.

Shauna didn't protest – she didn't have the energy. She hated being cooped up. The chickens were free to roam, but no, the doctor said she had to take it easy for a few days. Even the Mockingbird was off limits. She would love some comfort food about now. A gingerbread latte, with that tiny little gingerbread cookie on the side, and a piece of Ada's sugar pie would lift her spirits, but she was held captive in confinement. Her ginger ale and brown-sugar breakfast cookie would have to do for now. She was antsy. She was counting on the pain pills to relieve her headache and relax her screaming muscles. They hadn't kicked in.

A text or call from Gabe would be nice, too, she thought. Everyone said he was fine, but she wanted to see him with her own two eyes. She hated not knowing. She shook her head to empty her thoughts. She was letting her guard down. She didn't come home for a Christmas romance. She needed to simplify her life, not complicate it. She needed calm not chaos. She remembered her therapist saying she needed to connect to her past to find her future. Was Gabe in her future?

Shauna detested confinement more than being ill. In Atlanta she'd felt imprisoned in her home while she waited out the lawyers for a settlement and avoided her abuser. She'd finally felt free when she came home for Christmas. Now the bonds of circumstances held her in custody again. The thought of all the work she needed to accomplish for the Giving Tree project filled her mind.

"I don't know how long I can take this." She picked up the cat and laid her on the end of the couch, threw the quilt off, and jumped up to get her laptop. That was a mistake. Alice meowed and watched as Shauna dizzyingly stumbled back to the couch and plopped back down, barely averting a fainting disaster.

"Whew! That was close. I guess I better listen to the doctor and rest."

Alice looked intently as Shauna talked, then the cat went back to licking and grooming the fur that had been mussed.

Shauna bemoaned her situation. Yesterday, she had been laughing with chickens and today, she was chatting with a cat. She needed more people in her life.

She drew the quilt up around her shoulders, and Alice fastidiously crawled back into her arms. Shauna picked up the remote from the coffee table and turned on the TV, hoping time would pass by quicker, or if she fell asleep, she could handle the confinement and *not knowing* about Gabe easier. The quilt was soft and comforting. A nice touch of the holiday season with different shapes and sizes of patchwork trees, handstitched by her gran. Shauna called it her patchwork forest. It reminded her of the mountains that cradled Spring Valley. Her Gran always said, "When you sleep under a quilt, you sleep under a cover of love." She felt comforted. She felt loved.

It was perfect timing. Her favorite soap opera, or, as Gran would call it, "her story" was broadcasting. Her mother never allowed the girls to watch soap operas when they were growing up. She felt the bedroom scenes were not for younger eyes. She was probably right about that, but she didn't know that Gran let them watch whenever they were visiting. It was hush-hush. During the bedroom scenes she would make the girls cover their eyes, just in case their mom discovered their little secret. Shauna started enjoying the soap opera. Gran said she had watched so long, they seemed like family. Shauna had to agree. But it wasn't the actors that made it special, it was the memories of sitting with Gran sharing their stories. She fell asleep to the purr of Alice, and Victor and Nicky arguing over a family squabble.

#

The loud DING from Shauna's text notification drew her out of her slumber. Her mom must have set the speaker as loud as it would go – it sounded like a gong. She hadn't had too many hangovers in her life, but this one was a doozy, and she didn't remember drinking. She reached for her forehead and it reminded her it wasn't alcohol causing the pain, but a crash.

Her eyes focused on the text. It was from Gabe.

Are you up for a visitor?

She fumbled a one-word response.

Sure.

The doorbell immediately rang. She held her ears to muffle the sound. She thought she would have time to change into real clothes. Instead of making him wait in the cold, she wrapped the quilt around her silly holiday snowmen pajamas, and shuffled over to the door.

She opened the door. And felt something inside her melt. Gabe greeted her with a dozen red roses. The universal symbol of love. It touched her heart. Did he know that or was that all the florist had available this morning? Either way, now she knew he was safe, and he was standing in her presence.

A feeling of total failing rushed over Gabe when he first saw Shauna. He thought of last night when she was so spirited at Mr. Barnett's home, bossing around men twice her age and size accomplishing their roofing tasks, helping Timmy decorate the tree, and making sure Mr. Barnett had a hand in what conspired in his home. She was a whirlwind. Now she was sluggish and as pale as a ghost. It had happened so quickly. One moment they were happy, celebrating the successful event, the next moment a collision. A head-on collision that could have been fatal. He tightly gripped the bouquet, averting his pent-up anger. Anger with himself.

She broke the ice by teasing him, "I thought you said you Northerners knew how to drive in a foot of snow."

He smiled.

She laughed. It made her head hurt. "Be on the lookout for those Tennessee clueless drivers," she mimicked his previous words and winked, pointing to the SUV in the driveway. "I see you got a new ride out of the deal."

"It's a rental, but I do like the idea of a new SUV."

"Come on in. Pardon my pajamas. I didn't know you were on my doorstep when you texted."

When she turned to walk back to the sofa, she steadied herself on the kitchen counter. Gabe quickly put his arm around her shoulders and led her to the sofa. It felt nice.

"Are you sure you're ready for visitors? I can leave if you want. I just had to see for myself that you were okay." He sat across from her on the accent chair beside the Christmas tree. Alice jumped off the couch to check out the guest.

The last thing Shauna wanted was for Gabe to leave. She was so confused. One minute she walks away from him, the next she wants him by her side.

"No, please stay for a few minutes."

She reached for Alice before she covered Gabe's pant leg in cat hair. She held Alice up toward his direction for a proper introduction. The cat went limp, and her legs dangled. "Alice, meet Gabe. Gabe, meet Alice." Alice squirmed out of her grip. Uninterested and unimpressed with this stranger in the house, she sprinted to the next room and sought sanctuary under the bed.

Gabe thought, she's a *cat* person. He had qualms how Big Papi would react.

"You poor thing." He wanted to gently run his thumb over the dark shadow under her eye. Erase the pain. Erase the trauma. "How do you feel?"

"I told my mom this morning that I felt like I had been run over by a truck." She sighed, then giggled. "She said I had." It was evident to her Gabe was moving slower than usual. "Enough about me. Bless your heart, how do you feel?"

"I'm sore. I have some bumps and bruises,

and ringing in my ears from the shotgun sound of the airbag deployment, but I'll be fine." She looked so fragile. "I am so sorry, Shauna."

His eyes were filled with sorrow and compassion. They comforted her.

Shauna assured him she didn't hold him responsible in any way. "There's no reason for you to be sorry. You didn't do anything. I was just teasing you about your driving skills." She asked, "Do you know what happened to the driver who hit us?"

"I just stopped by the hospital, to inquire about his condition. At first they wouldn't release any information, but I asked if they would call and see if he would allow me to visit, miraculously he gave his consent."

Shauna thought he must have used his extraordinary persuasion skills again. "I'm learning you're really good at sweet talking."

"I prefer the term, *negotiator*." He grinned and studied her pale face. Her brilliant eyes, red hair, and the pink bandage on her head gave her porcelain complexion color. "He had a broken collarbone. They wanted to keep him a few days, but he's going to be fine." Gabe took off his coat and settled in as he spoke. "He feels awful. He wanted me to assure you that he was sorry. He hit black ice and lost control around the curve."

He didn't tell her that last night, while in the waiting room, he wanted to find the guy in the hospital and punch his lights out. But after he was assured Shauna would have a full recovery, his anger had calmed, and he allowed forgiveness to enter his heart.

Gabe wanted to hold Shauna, he wanted to caress her face, but instead, sat back in the chair to keep him from reaching and cradling her in his arms. "The police report showed he wasn't under the influence, but in the eyes of the insurance company, he will be at fault. I've already contacted my insurance agent and emailed the police report."

"You've been busy this morning. I've managed to get chauffeured home and nap. I feel nonproductive." She grinned.

"Shauna, I think we need to let someone else take care of the ACHIEVE Christmas wish." He spoke short and to the point.

She protested, "Absolutely not. We have enough time to pull it off. I may be in confinement, but I can still make calls and text."

"But the doctor said you needed plenty of rest to recover."

"This project is near and dear to your heart." She wanted him to know that she listened and remembered when he shared his childhood memories of his mother. "Give me another twenty-four hours and we'll have a day of planning."

"Are you sure twenty-four hours is enough?" He didn't want to alarm her, but she didn't look up for the task. "Let's make it forty-eight hours."

"Okay, forty-eight hours. I'll rest and I'll recover. We can get it done, we're a team."

We're a team. He liked the sound of that. He abandoned his idea of relinquishing the task to another.

"I saw a t-shirt in a catalog that said, 'Never underestimate the power of a stubborn redhead.' I'm guessing, you're stubborn," he teased.

She frowned and looked at him under her furrowed brow. "For your information, I may have been called stubborn a few more times than I can count, but I don't think it has anything to do with my hair color." She stroked her waterfall braid.

All of a sudden, referring to her hair made her self-conscious of her post-hospital presentation. "I'm definitely not a sight for sore eyes, today. You probably wanted to run when the door opened. Mom tried to dab all the crusty blood out of my hair this morning and salvaged my braid, but, today, this is good as it gets."

There was nothing that would make him want to run. "I've got to admit, I think the bandage is kind of sexy."

She laughed. "Then I may have to keep it as an accessory."

Chapter Seventeen

T he second day is always the worst. He could attest to that. He had experienced the phenomenon after intense workouts. His trainer always assured him it was natural. He called it DOMS – delayed onset of muscular soreness. Gabe wondered what he would call this circumstance. He came up with DOMC – delayed onset of motor collision. The discomfort from an intense workout didn't come close to the pain and tear in his muscles he experienced now. He wasn't a wimp, but he felt like one this morning. He could only imagine how Shauna must feel. He knew he needed to move to help relieve his sore muscles; he couldn't just sit around and feel sorry for himself. Active recovery was greatly needed.

He sat on the edge of the bed, rubbed Big Papi on the head and asked, "Hey, buddy, how about a hike?"

That perked him up. He jumped off the bed and headed downstairs to the kitchen door. It never ceased to amaze Gabe that his pup understood "how about a hike?". Whether he associated it with the particular behavior that followed, he wasn't sure. But he knew Big Papi loved the mountains as much as he did.

He would text Shauna on the way to the trail and let her know he would arrive early afternoon. She had said she would be up for planning, but he wasn't so sure. He didn't want to push her physically or emotionally. He was perplexed. He thought it might be easier if he were in a sparring match with an old flame of Shauna's, instead of his competitor being her past; the fears and anxieties that wouldn't let go. Fear had a tight grip on her, he hoped he could help her pry it loose. His instinct was to rescue her, he wanted nothing more, but he knew he couldn't. That was up to her. He could believe, listen, support her. He could help her heal. Recovery was a long road, he had to let her move at her pace. He decided he was going to ask her how he could help, and hope for an answer. He felt helpless.

The massaging showerhead sent a stream of hot pulsating water beads, easing his sore muscles. As the steam filled the shower his mind relaxed and drifted to thoughts of Shauna. This petite ginger spitfire – her strength astonished him. Sexual harassment cases were in the media spotlight. He read the articles describing how most victims feel powerless, terrified, or intimidated to confront their attacker. They choose to stay quiet and hide their secret. Shauna chose to take her power back and expose her abuser for what he truly was.

The aftermath from publicly exposing the harassment, the restraining order, and the drawn-out legal action that followed almost broke her. His anger boiled, just thinking about it. But from what he witnessed; she was slowly gluing the pieces of her life back together.

He stepped out of the shower, towel-dried his hair and tied a towel around his waist. While his hair was damp, he ran his hands through his mane with a dab of conditioner. He could hear the TV he had left on in the bedroom blaring the morning news. When the headline hits close to home, it takes on a whole new perspective.

Big Papi had been patiently waiting at the kitchen-entrance rug. Gabe attached his leash to the collar and opened the door. Big Papi came to an abrupt stop to sniff the unexpected gift basket someone had placed on the welcome mat. Just as the dog lifted his leg to mark his territory and claim ownership, Gabe rescued the basket from destruction.

"Whoa, Big Papi!" He pulled on the leash, and escorted Big Papi back to the kitchen.

He unwrapped the gift and found two loaves of warm, freshly baked banana nut bread from his neighbors, the Barkleys. The note read: *So sorry to hear about your accident. Praying for a swift recovery.* Included was a dog biscuit.

"Look, boy, they didn't forget you!" Big Papi snatched it out of his hand and started chomping. Gabe cut a slice of the bread and devoured it.

Gabe had to admit he loved Southern hospitality. It was warm, sweet, and always welcome.

#

First thing in the morning, making the bed was the norm. It was one of her "depression busters" the therapist had suggested. A motivational tool to carry throughout the day. *If you're faithful in small things, it's easier to focus on the big things.* Today, Shauna knew her therapist would let her off the hook if the bed wasn't made perfectly. She somehow managed to pull the quilt up over the wrinkled, lumpy sheets. She read the wall plaque posted over the headboard. *Yes, my soul finds rest in God; my hope comes from him.* She smiled. It was just wall decor, but this morning it was as if Gran had left her a simple Psalms Post-it note. She smiled. It was a lovely reminder.

She was relieved when she read Gabe's text letting her know he would arrive in the afternoon. Her mind had deceived her with the erroneous idea she would rise for an early morning. Everything ached. Her body called out for relief. She prescribed herself a long, relaxing bath in volcanos of bubbles. She filled the freestanding, deep soaker tub. She was happy her parents had made the upgrade when they added this luxury item. For work, she usually showered, it always jumpstarted her brain for planning the day. The bath, she reserved for quiet meditation.

She tied up her curls in a messy topknot, sunk down slowly in the steamy hot water, and stopped at the perfect spot for support for her aching back, neck, and head. Today, the water felt silkier from the Epsom salts she'd added to relax her sore muscles and stress tension. Settled, she closed her eyes for a blissful thirty minutes. She focused on one thing, her breathing. She took slow, deep breaths and cleared her mind. Her body relaxed.

When the water cooled, she lifted the release and let the water down the drain, and slowly stood, supporting herself with the high edge of the tub. The bath salts were a great relief, but not a magical cure. That would take time.

She flipped on the exhaust fan to clear the fogged mirror. As the mist evaporated, her reflection appeared. Since the accident, she had tried to avoid mirrors. The pink bandage forewarned of what lay beneath. A scar that would now be part of her facial features. The doctor had assured her it would be barely visible – she could only hope. She had enough invisible scars to last a lifetime.

She could see why her family worried and why this new man in her life felt the need to protect her. Unclothed, she looked fragile and weak. The bruises accentuated her fragility. *You are courageous, you are strong* drifted in her mind.

She was courageous. She felt stronger. She sensed she was halfway home. She knew, from experience, the worst part of running a half marathon wasn't the starting point or the finish line. It was the middle – the halfway point. On her first attempt at the test of endurance, she almost quit. The excruciating pain of side stitches screamed for her to stop. Her lungs gasped for air; her legs almost buckled. Everything in her body told her to quit, drop out, you're too weak. Her brain refused to listen, she trotted on in pain, rose above circumstances, and conquered as she crossed the finish line.

She was more than halfway home to reclaiming her life. Each step brought her closer to overcoming adversity.

#

After dressing, Shauna stared indecisively at the coffee maker. Colleen had left an assortment of coffee pods, but Shauna knew it would be a mistake to just sit around. She needed to at least get in a short walk to the main house. It would help improve her blood flow and speed up healing. She was all-in for that. The bath had relieved her muscles but not enough to struggle with the sleeves of her coat, she opted to just wrap herself in the quilt she had left draped over the back of the couch, slipped her feet in clogs, and shuffled to the house.

She punched in the door code, 1225, and let herself in.

"Good morning! What are you doing out roaming around?" Colleen was surprised to see her daughter up and moving. "You should have called; I would have come running. You shouldn't be doing too much, too soon."

"I know you would, Mom, you've been great. If you remember, the doctor cleared me to move around. She said I needed rest to recover, but I also needed to be mobile."

"Just don't do too much." Colleen couldn't help but worry. "Your dad picked up some pastries this morning from the Mockingbird. I was just getting ready to deliver one to you on my way to work."

Shauna poured a cup of coffee and noticed the smooth river rock engraved with the word "joy" that sat on the counter beside the coffee maker. "Mom, I've seen this little rock in the kitchen before but never asked about it. Did someone give it to you?"

"No, I bought that for myself." She had kept the story of the rock a secret from Shauna. She thought maybe today would be the day to reveal it. "It's just a daily reminder."

"A reminder for what?"

"When you were a senior in high school, your dad and I went through a very difficult time in our marriage, we even considered divorce." Colleen didn't disclose the reasons for the troubled marriage, it didn't matter now, forgiveness ended the blame and left it in the past.

Shauna's eyes widened in disbelief. "I had no

THE ORNAMENT OF HOPE

idea." She was beyond shocked to think divorce was ever mentioned. "I'm sorry, Mom, I knew you argued, but you actually contemplated divorce?"

"We tried to hide it from you. The last year in high school is the stepping-stone to college. It's so important, we didn't want to spoil it for you. So we fought behind closed doors and kept our distance from each other."

Shauna sat in the high wingback chair tucked in the kitchen nook, feeling guilty that she had been so caught up building a life for her future, she hadn't noticed that her parents' lives were falling apart. "What happened? What saved your marriage?"

"That's a long story, for another day. Let me answer the rock question first." Colleen walked over and picked up the rock and stood at the kitchen sink to tell the rest of the story.

"I didn't want a divorce. I cried every day for over a year. One afternoon after work, I stopped in the convenience store to pick up a few items. On the way home, I started tearing up again, and prayed out loud to God. I remember pleading that I just wanted my joy back." She caressed the little rock in her hand. "As soon as those words came out of my mouth, a big dog ran out in front of the car. I slammed on the brakes, just in time to miss the dog. My groceries tumbled to the floor except for one item that landed in my lap."

Colleen bent down to open the counter under the sink to retrieve a bottle of dish liquid. Shauna thought it odd that she was concerned with washing dishes at a time like this.

"The one item that landed in my lap was a bottle of Joy." She held up the dish liquid. "I laughed through my tears. I got my joy back. God plopped it smack dab in my lap. After that day, I chose to choose joy, no matter what the circumstance. These are my daily reminders to choose joy." She sat the rock and the dish liquid together on the counter. "Remember the story in the Bible when the woman caught in adultery was thrown at the feet of Jesus for his condemnation. Instead he looked at the crowd and said, 'He who has no sin, cast the first stone.' The rocks started thumping on the ground as the crowd dispersed. Jesus looked at the woman, and said those astounding words, 'Your sins are forgiven.' When I saw this rock in a little gift shop, I dropped my rock of condemnation and picked up a rock of forgiveness. Your father and I chose forgiveness and joy."

"Why no divorce?"

"After we moved you into your college dorm, our excuse to stay together for our child flew out the car window on the ride home. In a way, it forced us to make a decision to either work it out or go our separate ways. We both agreed to couples counseling and it saved our marriage. It helped us talk through the losses in our relationship. We found hope and loving solutions that eventually healed our relationship." She smiled through tears. "I can't believe I'm saying these words, because that year was beyond miserable, but almost losing our marriage was the best thing that ever happened to it. We're stronger than we've ever been and I love your dad more now, than ever."

Shauna held a newfound utmost respect for her mother. Her mom's inspirational words, *choose joy*, tugged her along the path of recovery.

Chapter Eighteen

S he was dressed when the doorbell rang. The comfy and warm lavender fleece top paired with terry jogger pants and fluffy socks were perfect for lounging around or, if need be, outdoor casual wear. After the fashion faux pas of greeting Gabe in her mother's selection of childish snowmen pajamas, she wanted to present a trendier mature look. Anything would be better than snowmen PJ's. She kept a cozy sherpa wrap handy to replace the quilt.

Her eyes brightened to see he was bearing gifts. A gingerbread latte accompanied by the little gingerbread-man cookie. Her favorite treat! She had to admit, she was more thrilled to see the delivery man.

He decided she was another paradigm of Southern hospitality. Warm, sweet, and a sight always welcomed.

"Well, for heaven's sakes, you're a mind reader!" She anxiously reached for the coffee as he entered the cottage.

"That's the only drink I've seen you order, so I thought it would be a safe choice."

"Perfect!" She licked the whipped cream topping and tasted a hint of cinnamon.

"You should probably try not to inhale the whipped cream." He took his thumb and cleaned her whipped cream smudged nose. She had this childlike spirit when it came to lattes. It was one of her most endearing qualities. His heart skipped a beat.

"How was the trail?"

"It was invigorating! Just what I needed. When you're up to it, we'll have to take a hike together." He tested the waters.

"When I'm up to it? Don't know when that will be, but when I'm ready, just don't plan a long hike. I told you, I'm a short day-hike kind of girl."

"I promise." He crossed his heart.

She set down her drink as she cleared the table. "I just finished a wrapping project. It arrived today and I wanted it concealed in case Paige visited with Abby after work." Shauna relocated the present to under the tree and freed up the coffee table for their planning session.

"If a stranger saw you and Paige walking down the street, they would assume she was your child. She's your Mini-Me."

"That's actually happened. We love it!" Shauna reached for her phone to show him a picture. "I bought this American Girl doll for her this year."

Gabe sat next to her on the couch to view the pic. "Is it custom made? It looks just how I imaged you as a little girl."

Realizing Gabe probably didn't have a clue about the dolls, she gave him a brief tutorial on the craze.

"The doll's name is Blaire and she's accompanied with her very own book that tells her history and every detail of her daily life. Get this. Not only is she our spitting image, she's a chicken wrangler. Just like Mom." She chuckled, then panicked. "Oh, no! I didn't let the chickens out of the coop this morning. I bet they are beyond annoyed." She fluttered her lashes and pouted her lip. "Would you do me a huge favor and open the coop?"

"I'm no chicken wrangler, but how hard could it be?" He headed out the door. He needed a quick escape from her pleading eyes and tempestuous perfect mouth.

She yelled out after him, "You're a life saver! Watch your step. There's chicken poop!"

She was pleased with herself that before Gabe arrived she had wrapped a couple of presents, prepared for their planning session, and hadn't felt the need to nap, but suddenly she realized she may have been doing too much, too soon. Just as her mother warned. The overwhelming need to shut her eyes took over. Her intent was to just rest her eyes for a few minutes while Gabe tended to the chickens.

The good intention proved to be a bad idea for Gabe. Her catnap evolved into a deep sleep.

She snored herself awake. She looked at the time. She had napped for forty minutes. She realized her visiting chicken wrangler had not returned. The coat rack still held his coat, so that was a relief. At least he didn't sneak in and find his sleeping beauty snoring and run for the hills. She went to the back window to view the coop. She discovered something she never could have envisioned.

Her ribs cried out in pain as she laughed at the sight. Gabe was hunched over in the coop with his newfound feathered friends pecking away around his feet. He had to be over six foot two, and the chicken coop height was five foot, at most. Somehow, he'd locked himself in. She grabbed her shawl to release him from chicken jail.

"It's about time. I'm freezing," he called out before Shauna could say a word. Fortunately, he managed a grin from behind the chicken wire. She was moving slow. He didn't want to rush her but he was freezing. His back muscles started to seize, for relief he squatted down. He tried to keep his balance, fearing if he tumbled in the mess, he would wipe out Santa's second string.

"I've been calling your name. I was hoping the goose whisperer you talked about would show up around the pond, but no such luck."

From all the excitement, she could swear the hens joined her in squawking laughter as they franticly pranced around, ruffling their feathers. She held her hand over her mouth, while she engaged in a futile skirmish with her laughter. Hoping for forgiveness, she tried locking eyes with the prisoner behind the wire, then remembered the warning that if you encountered a black bear, you should not make eye contact. The bear would perceive it as an act of aggression. The laugher she tried to suppress must have gone straight to her brain. It pumped out ideas for a comedy routine. Under the circumstance, the best comparison wasn't a bear, but Big Bird. She unlatched the gate to let her big bird out of the cage.

"I am so sorry. I closed my eyes to take a catnap, but needless to say..." She couldn't hold it in any longer and burst out laughing. "I am so sorry," she repeated.

"It's not your fault. I somehow locked myself in." He stretched his arms out in front of his body, clasped one hand on top of the other and gently reached out as he felt his shoulder blades stretching away from each other, bending his head forward to relieve his seized muscles.

"I can take some of the blame. That door locks from the outside."

"I'm aware of that, now. My hand is too large to lift the latch from the inside. I left my wallet in the car, so I didn't even have a thin credit card to lift the latch, and my phone is in my jacket, in the cottage."

Shauna meekly pointed. "There's a handle on the outside of the coop that releases the little door on their house. You didn't need to go inside."

"Well, I was not aware of that tidbit of information."

She doubled over in laughter again, holding her sides. "If you knew just how bad it hurts for me to laugh, you would realize how hilarious you look."

"So, you're going with the, 'it hurts me more than it does you' catchphrase?" he murmured. "I'm just thankful, beyond measure, that you released me before you thought to snap a selfie. This ridiculous scene would be captured forever." He shivered from the cold.

She giggled; her brain was on a roll. "It gives *freeze frame*, a whole new meaning." She pulled her phone out of her pocket.

In a flash, Gabe snatched the phone out of her hand, scooped her up in his arms, and carried her back to the cottage. She didn't protest.

Before he carried her over the threshold she demanded, "Wait, put me down!"

Contemplating her sudden appeal, he questioned his gallant move. Was her protest in fear? Anger? Was everything happening too fast? He lowered her feet to the porch to let her stand on her own.

"Your boots are covered in chicken poop." She scrunched her face. "I'm sure you need both hands to remove them." He was relieved and amused.

Watching her in the doorway, Gabe unlaced his boots and pulled them off and left them on the porch; trusting a stray dog wouldn't nab his boots. He laughed. He thought of how chicken poop would now be a part of their story.

#

Shauna offered Gabe a peace treaty, a cup of hot cocoa. They began their afternoon of planning. The memories of the day at Mr. Barnett's hadn't faded, and they fueled their task at hand. Timmy's wish had inspired hope, not only in Gabe and Shauna, but in volunteers who willingly gave so freely to help fulfill it. The accident had slowed them down, but didn't discourage their determination to grant another wish.

"I would really like to have this event somewhere special for the kids. What do you think about booking the community room at the Train Depot?" asked Gabe.

"I think that's a fantastic idea," Shauna enthusiastically agreed. "Let's book Santa for the evening."

Gabe shook his head. "I don't know, he's probably booked solid."

"Remember, I know him personally, he can help us pull off a Christmas miracle," she assured him.

He liked the way she talked.

"We know from the wish list, they need a small gift for each child, a craft ornament, and some fun little things to do at the party." Shauna rubbed her finger over her chapped bottom lip and pulled out the drawer under the coffee table to retrieve her chap stick. As she rolled it on, she mumbled, "Abby has already volunteered to help with the ornaments and we can manage overseeing the cookie-decorating table."

"This may be a crazy idea, but I could buy a baseball glove and ball for each of the children. I think that's a safe unisex gift, don't you?" Gabe asked, reflecting on the prized baseball glove his mother had placed under the tree when he was six. That was the only present she could afford that Christmas.

"Yes, I think that's a splendid idea, but you can't. You know the rules." She wagged a finger at him. "We are the facilitators. Our job is to get as many people as we can to make this wish come true."

"You're right. I don't want to be on Ada's bad side. I was just trying to cut corners, since the accident robbed some of our time."

"Trust me, I've known Ada all my life, she doesn't have a bad side."

"Okay, what about this idea? It's hard for single moms to purchase gifts at Christmas. How about having a toy room where they can choose a gift for their child, wrap it, and when they go home, they'll have a gift to place under the tree."

"I love that idea! Their own personal Toy Boutique." He melted her heart. She knew he spoke from his own experiences.

"Merchants offer free wrapping for the holiday; I'll see if we can get them involved." Gabe volunteered for that task. Being on the town council had its perks.

"I'll contact Mrs. Bowman from ACHIEVE and ask for the age and gender of each child, and I'll use Abby's Facebook page to get the word out for donated gifts. We can use the Christmas shop as the drop-off location."

"Everyone loves pizza. That's an easy menu."

"Don't forget the potato chips." He gave her a weird look. "It's a Southern thing, you can't eat pizza without chips," she explained as she stood and went to the kitchen cabinet to retrieve pain pills.

"Also, the decorated cookies will serve two purposes. A craft and dessert."

"Perfect! There's another tradition I would like to add." She returned to the couch and put her hands together pleading. "I know this will sound super weird, but every year in my stocking there's an apple, an orange, a few nuts to crack, and a peppermint stick of candy."

"Okay, that is a little strange."

"My grandparents remembered a time when gifts were minimal. Money was always in short supply; however, their families always found a way to make the holiday special. Children in the mountain communities found stockings hung by their beds on Christmas morn, filled with fruit, nuts, and candy. Back in the day it was a rare treat in Appalachia and, at times, their only gift. My parents carry on the tradition to connect us to our heritage, and to remind us that simple gifts given with love are the most precious."

Gabe was beginning to appreciate her stories of long ago and this simple approach to the holidays in a more cluttered world. He may have just discovered the reason for Shauna's disdain for commercializing Christmas, but chose to share his analysis at a later date.

"When my neighbor, Mrs. Barkley, heard through the grapevine that I had volunteered for The Giving Tree, she offered to help. I'll see if she would like to gather the fruit, candy, and nuts." Gabe was thinking of Mr. Barkley and his possible Alzheimer's diagnosis, as he knew recent memories are mostly lost. He hoped a happy memory from his childhood might be preserved and would bring joy, and Mr. and Mrs. Barkley could reminisce past Christmases together, one more year.

"Mrs. Barkley is just the sweetest thing. You won't have to explain the tradition to her. She's living proof – she could school you. There are a few churches out in the country that still give out bags of fruit, with oranges and apples, at the close of their Christmas play. She may know the pastors and could ask if they had a few extra bags of treats to spare." Shauna let out a long sigh and started massaging her temples. "My brain is tired!"

He brushed back a tousled hair that had fallen in front of her eye. She leaned her head on his shoulder and yawned.

"You need a quick nap before your sister arrives." He kissed her on the top of her head, scooted off the couch, and she rested her head on the pillow.

"Excuse me if I don't show you to the door."

"I think I can find it, it's only about ten feet away," he teased. "Before you pass out, would you like me to cook dinner for you Friday night? I need to break in my new kitchen stove."

"I'll agree if you agree to joining me and my family Thursday night for the twins' Christmas play. It will be my first night out since the wreck, I'll need someone big and strong to lean on."

"It's a deal. I would love to escort you to the play." He could tell she was getting punchy as the pain pills kicked in. It didn't matter, she'd said she needed him.

#

Shauna had a delightfully delicious assortment of baked goods to choose from for breakfast. The night before, Abby and Paige had hauled in gifts from well-wishers who heard through the small-town grapevine of the accident and Shauna's injuries. Whether she wanted to admit it or not, she was one of them. They were her people. It warmed her heart.

Bundling up for a short morning stroll on the walking trail, Shauna set her own ground rules, and limited herself to not going beyond the pond. Benches were stationed around the path, in case she needed to rest. Before she left the warmth of the cottage, she gave her fur baby one last pat on her soft little noggin. Alice meowed her goodbye, jumped off the couch, and meandered to her bowl on the kitchen floor, giving Shauna a squinted cat-eyed look with the attitude of preferring to be served breakfast in bed.

Shauna wasn't allowed to run as she was recovering from a concussion, but she needed to move. She needed to think. She was still processing the secret. The mind-boggling secret that at one point in time her parents' marriage teetered on the brink of divorce. She was befuddled. If her mother had shared more details, maybe she could understand the reasoning behind why their marriage was so desperate that they considered ending it. She couldn't imagine them not being together. Living separate lives. They were the foundation of her family.

She whispered a prayer of thanks for her parents' miracle of overcoming struggles. Choosing joy and love over judgment. They found hope in hopelessness. The power of love endured.

She wanted that. Sustaining hope. An enduring love. A lasting love. A love that would stand the test of time.

The brisk, cool air made her feel alive. She strolled around the pond for a few minutes. Tiring, she took refuge on a bench that sat next to the giant bare willow with its branches dangling over the pond. Stripped of its leaves, its color; resting in winter, preparing for new bold life in spring.

Rest, Shauna thought as she watched the calming ripples of the water, she herself was resting in winter. Preparing for her spring.

She watched a pair of geese, with their built-in insulating downy feathers, waddle off the winter-brown grassy bank, murmuring occasional honks as they braved the cold water, gliding effortlessly, moving as if they were King and Queen of the pond.

"Good morning!"

Shauna startled. She'd thought she was alone. She turned to see the woman she recognized as the goose whisperer. She stood directly behind her bench, in Shauna's personal space. It was a little unsettling.

"Good morning to you," Shauna replied. She surmised the woman had completed her rule-breaking, fowl-feeding ritual earlier, and returned to enjoy the solitude of the park.

"They're so beautiful. I just love watching." Not allowing for a response from Shauna, she said, "They've been a couple for years. Geese are monogamous. They are fiercely committed to each other, but if one dies, they find another mate." Shauna found her attitude was very matter-of-fact, considering she'd just spoken of lovers.

"I didn't realize they mated for life." Shauna gestured to the cottage, peeking through the space between the evergreen trees, once planted for privacy. "My gran lived in that cottage for a few years, before she passed. She spent hours sitting on this very bench. Just thinking and watching."

"I met your gran. She was a lovely lady." She was direct and to the point, leaving Shauna wondering how well she knew her grandmother.

"Thank you, she was."

"I've seen you on the trail, recently. You're usually running. Do you live in the cottage now?"

Not wanting to divulge her life's story, Shauna abbreviated her answer. "I'm home visiting for the holidays. But I'm considering moving back."

The woman smiled and nodded her head. "You sound like the goslings. They always return home to their birthplace."

Maybe too somberly, Shauna replied, "Is that so?"

"Well, I'm sorry if I disturbed you. I'll mosey on along."

The woman left, just as quietly as she came, leaving Shauna deep in thought, mulling over the woman's words. *If one dies, they find another mate... They always return home to their birthplace.*

Maybe she had been too quick to judge and had jumped to the unwarranted conclusion that the goose whisperer was a nuisance by feeding the fowl. She seemed to be more of a guardian. Maybe their conversation was more than idle chatter. Maybe, just maybe, their meeting wasn't a coincidence but a *Godincidence*. Was she foolish to think that Gabe might be the one? Would she ever be content living in Spring Valley?

When she'd walked out the door for a little exercise, she had hoped she would find clarity on her morning stroll. Confusion followed her back to the cottage.

Chapter Nineteen

It took longer than the time she allotted for dressing for the Christmas play. She was definitely on the mend, but still moved slow. It was to be her first official time out of the house since the accident, and she wanted to join the family and Gabe for this special Christmas celebration at church. She had several dresses laid out on the bed to choose from. She loved the way emerald green accented her hair, but decided she didn't want to be mistaken for Christmas garland. After wasting time on a personal fashion show, she made her choice. She wore her favorite royal-blue, form-fitting sweater dress. She was a little alarmed when she caught her reflection. She had been wearing casual, oversized, bulky clothing the last few months and hadn't bothered to step on the scales. The mirror didn't lie, the dress didn't fit as snugly as the last time she wore it. Maybe her mom was right, she was almost skin and bones. She was happy her appetite had returned, maybe soon she would be back to her normal weight. She wore her hair down and let her curls fall on her shoulders. The bandage on her forehead added a little pink punch to the ensemble and served as a friendly reminder she was still on the mend.

It had been a long time since her family had filled a pew. She had always sat next to Gran. That spot that had been empty for several years, to-night, would be reserved for Gabe.

"Gabriel." She spoke his name out loud, just to hear the sound of it. Her gran would have like his name, the angel Gabriel was God's messenger of hope. Maybe he was her Christmas angel. A tin-gle went up her spine.

Touching up her cinnamon lipstick, she heard the doorbell ring and blotted her lips. Be-fore greeting her date, she grabbed her coat and purse. She opened the door.

Her stomach swam with butterflies. Did he have to look so ruggedly handsome?

"You clean up good."

"You look absolutely radiant!" Gabe thought of how her color choice intensified her sapphire eyes that dazzled like jewels.

In her playful way, she struck a model pose. "I'm ready for the catwalk."

Taking a step inside, he reached for her coat to help his lady with her frock. She obliged. She liked that he'd adopted these Southern customs. He kissed her gently on the cheek, took her by the hand, and led her to her chariot parked in the drive.

"Will you be able to join our family at Mom and Daddy's for dessert and coffee?"

"I would love to!" He opened the door for her as she gingerly lifted herself onto the high SUV seat. As she strapped the seat belt on, he leaned in and said, "Maybe they will tell some great embarrassing childhood stories about you." He winked and closed the door.

#

After the play, as Abby, Tyler, and the kids dashed home to change before joining the rest of the family, Shauna and Gabe took a slow tour through her parents' house, while her mom prepared the dessert. The homespun holiday decorations served as a perfect accent to the Americana interior design. Their home reflected their family and cultural roots through the primitive folk art displayed throughout the house. Each one-of-a-kind piece had a story that evoked a memory of the past. As they went from room to room, Shauna describing the pieces and her people was as natural as if flipping through an old photo album.

She picked up one of the ornaments that resembled Mr. Barnett's. "This is one of my daddy's favorite pieces. It was the first piece he and his grandpaw whittled together when he was a little boy, barely old enough to hold a knife." She had heard the stories so many times, she could visualize her father as a little boy, sitting on the front porch whittling with his grandpaw. The rudimentary carved bear was the work of a novice child, but it was priceless to her father. It was more than a piece of carved wood; it was a memory etched in his heart.

Gabe's mind was befuddled when he came

across incongruous modernized pieces mixed in with the old-fashioned folk-art furniture. He hadn't expected the combination but, somehow, it worked; Colleen had effortlessly combined elements from both. The simplicity of the folk art took on a contemporary aspect and blended naturally with modern pieces. He was amazed by the symbolism. Artifacts of the past, balancing the present.

"How do you know so much about your family? You're like an Ancestry.com walking commercial," Gabe teased.

"Living with heirlooms keeps the past, present." She turned to smile at Gabe.

His knowledge of his family heritage was minuscule. She made him to want to know more about his ancestry. He desired a stronger connection to his roots.

Christmas pictures of Shauna and Abby were displayed on the dining-room table. Before he caught a glimpse, she tried to conceal them with her body, but it was of no use. He picked up a framed photo to see Shauna in all of her toothless glory, sitting on Santa's lap. It made her laugh to see her six-year-old self in a ridiculous grin.

"You're adorable!" He admired the younger, innocent version of Shauna, when the only care in the world was sharing her list with old Saint Nick.

She grabbed the picture out of his hand and hid it behind her back. "I was hoping you wouldn't see that."

She chose a poor hiding place; her waist was tiny compared to his long arms. He snuggled up against her and reached around to retrieve the picture, locking his arms softly around her waist, so not to aggravate her aches and pains. He wanted to kiss her, but resisted his urge. If he had known their last kiss had lingered in her mind, and she dreamed of another, he would have indulged. Shauna laughed as she tried to playfully squirm out of his embrace. She didn't make a convincing effort.

Colleen had not heard her daughter laugh so freely in ages. She looked at Ryan and they both raised their eyebrows in curiosity. Ryan gave his wife the thumbs up. They had spent many hours praying their daughter would find peace and true happiness. Gabe seemed to make her happy.

The pop of the wine cork startled Shauna, she jumped and laughed again. "I think that's our cue to join them for a glass of bubbly." She took him by the hand and led him to the kitchen.

Ryan poured the adult drinks and prepared cocoa for the grandkids. As the guests of honor arrived, Colleen ran over to the twins and gave them a big congratulatory hug, and everyone else applauded. Paige and Bryce took a bow.

Shauna high-fived them. Her ribs weren't ready for big hugs. "Bryce, you were the best wise man on stage." Bryce still nobly wore his handmade mosaic crown.

"Paige, you were the most beautiful angel

on the stage! That was always my favorite character to play. But I think you're a better actress than
me."

Paige couldn't help but give her auntie a
gentle hug.

"Who's ready for dessert?" Colleen's question was answered by raised hands that shot up in
the air. "Come on over and grab a plate."

As they sat near the cozy fireplace in the
family room, chatting and nibbling on Colleen's
Southern Jam Cake, Abby prompted Shauna, "Remember that Christmas we almost had to call the
fire department to get your knee unstuck from the
railing?"

"Let's move on to another topic."

"No, no, no. I was hoping for an embarrassing story, tell me more." Gabe eyes twinkled with
mischief.

"I'll tell if you don't, Shauna, so you might as
well," Abby threatened.

"Okay." She relented. "Keep in mind I was
five years old."

"Wait, wait, let me set the staging." Abby
went into her dramatic storytelling voice. "The
electricity of excitement filled the pine-scented
air. The church, decked with boughs of holly, was
filled to capacity as moms, dads, grandparents,
aunts, and uncles flocked to see their little cher-
ubs perform."

"You sound more like a ringmaster at a cir-
cus, than a storyteller." Shauna laughed. "I'll fin-

ish."

Tyler leaned over and warned Gabe, "They're a little rowdy when they get together. Especially if they've had a little too much wine." He raised his glass and tipped it to his mouth.

Gabe loved every minute of it.

"Our time finally came, and my Sunday school class lined up on stage. Our teacher, Miss Millie, instructed us to stay right beside the rail that outlined the stage. All went smoothly as we recited memory verses and caroled, until it happened."

The kids sat and listened with anticipation. "What happened, Auntie Shauna? What happened?"

"Well, I admit, I was a little nervous and wriggling around, but obeyed my teacher and stayed really close to the rail. When we finished and the class turned to leave, I couldn't move. All my little friends passed me by, and I stood there, alone."

"We thought it was stage fright. If was as if her feet were frozen to the ground," Ryan chimed in.

She shook her head. "No, somehow I had wedged my knee between the rail slats and I was stuck."

Abby couldn't hold her laughter in, just like she and the rest of the audience did twenty-two years ago. Snickering rippled through the audience and within seconds turned into a wave of laughter.

Shauna giggled thinking about the scene. "Not only was I stuck, I was frightened and humiliated."

Colleen added, "We should have sent it in to *America's Funniest Home Videos*, it would have won ten thousand dollars and helped pay for your college tuition."

"If everyone would quit interrupting, I can get this over with and we can move on," Shauna bantered.

"Anyways, I looked out into the audience and found my parents. My eyes met Daddy's eyes and that's all it took. He jumped up and came to my rescue, just like I knew he would."

Getting up for a coffee refill, as he passed by, her dad leaned over and kissed her on the hair. "I thought I was going to have to go home and retrieve a hand saw to cut you out. It took a few minutes, but with more intentional wriggling, we set you free." That was one of many times he came to her rescue.

Witnessing Ryan adore his children, Gabe had a twinge of sadness. Where was his father? he wondered. Was he alive or dead? He usually kept those thoughts locked away, but tonight they tried to escape. He pushed them back in and enjoyed this family that welcomed him in their home.

Shauna quickly wrapped up the story. "The laughter faded... blah, blah, blah. The rest of the play went without a hitch. The end. Move on."

Gabe reached his arm around her shoulders as they sat snuggled on the couch. "That's exactly what I was looking forward to, you made my evening."

They all took turns revealing more embarrassing childhood stories.

Shauna basked in attention and cherished being surrounded by the ones she loved. It was just what she needed. She kept thinking of that night, as a child, when she was stuck in the railing. It was the same feeling she had felt before she came home from Atlanta. Stuck in her pageant of life. Frozen, alone, humiliated, unable to move forward. She felt like she had nowhere to turn. Tonight, was a far cry from that experience.

Shauna hadn't shared her spiritual moment she had experienced earlier that evening at church. A wellspring of peace poured out of her soul, giving her a sense of freedom. As she sat next to Gabe in the pew, she looked to the stained-glass window, an image depicting her Heavenly Father with an outstretched hand. She gazed into his eyes. They were only colored glass, but somehow they seemed real, loving, compassionate eyes. She silently prayed her Heavenly Father would come to her rescue. Her fears diminished. She recalled the scripture that Abby had texted to encourage her: *Be brave, be strong. Don't give up. God will be here soon.* In her thunderstorm, she wondered where He was and what He was waiting for. Tonight, she found the answer. He was there all the time. He was waiting for her. Waiting for her to call out. To surrender all to Him.

#

Colleen could see that her baby daughter was fading fast and she needed to wrap up their little get-together so Shauna could get back to the cottage and rest. It was a lot of activity for her first night out since the accident.

"We need to get these little rug rats home in bed. They've got a big day tomorrow helping Nana in the shop."

Not wanting to leave all the fun, the kids grumbled and complained. Shauna and Gabe lingered on the couch as a flurry of activity commenced getting the twins out the door. They said their goodbyes with hugs all around.

She looked at Gabe and asked, "Would you like to walk me to the cottage?"

"There's nothing I would like better than walking under the stars with a beautiful woman." He gave her his hand.

The air was crisp and smelled of burned wood from the smoke carried in the air from fireplace chimneys and woodburning stoves in the neighborhood. It conjured up a recent memory. The night around the firepit. The night they first kissed. They walked toward the cottage on the brick-lined pathway that sparkled like tiny diamonds from the frost. The cottage was close. The walk to the cottage porch was too brief.

Despite the unpleasantness from her aching muscles, the sweetness of his gentle goodnight kiss eased her discomfort. The perfect distraction.

"I better let you go. You need your rest." He drew her away and kissed her one last time on her brow. He promised he would text in the morning.

She obeyed, only because she was afraid she would faint from exhaustion if she didn't lie down. She leaned against the door and watched as he walked away. Tonight, she looked forward to her dreams.

Chapter Twenty

Big Papi alerted Gabe before the doorbell. He glanced up and saw Shauna at the back-kitchen entrance and motioned her to enter.

"Welcome to my humble kitchen."

Gabe's low, rich voice always soothed her nerves. The voice of a smooth-talking late-night DJ in some old movie.

The inn's kitchen was anything but humble. The twenty-first-century renovation upgrades sparkled with new state-of-the-art appliances, marble countertops, white glass front cabinets on the wall, with ample cabinetry on the bottom. Antique copper ceiling tiles swept eyes upward to the copper fixture hanging. She noticed he'd honored the inn's roots by reclaiming any wood that had survived the fire to use as open wood shelving. The circa 1790 double-basket-weave brick floor was recreated with look-alike deep-red tile. Her father had delivered the restored fireplace mantle with its ornate columns and deep rich wood the day before. It was the focal point of the room, framing a glowing fireplace, setting a romantic tone for the evening.

"This kitchen is incredible!" Shauna ran her hand over the cabinets, the smooth countertops, and progressed her way to the walk-in pantry. She pushed her way in through the swinging door then pushed the other way out to see Gabe. "You've got to be kidding me. Look at the size of this pantry." Shauna paused her tour for a moment. "This would be the envy of any chef. Good grief, you could set up housekeeping in here."

She was too occupied exploring and didn't notice she had a furry friend tracing her every step until, on the way out of the pantry, Big Papi got tangled up in her feet and let out a yelp.

With his chef's knife at work, Gabe looked like a pro. "Give me a second, I'm chopping some fresh rosemary and thyme for the herb lemon butter, then I'll relocate Big Papi to the bedroom. Otherwise, he'll be at your feet all night." A strand of his thick hair flopped on his forehead. She wanted to reach over and brush it back, but resisted.

He cleaned his hands on the apron he had tied around his waist and turned his attention to the task at hand. "Big Papi. Let's go." The dog immediately followed him through the door.

Left alone, Shauna noticed the smell of the sea – lobster to be exact. The sight of such an unexpected and amazing kitchen must have overpowered her other senses. Her tastebuds sent messages to her brain to run. She went to the stove and started sniffing. She reached for a pot holder to check out what was under the lid.

"No peeking!" Gabe caught her in the act.

She dropped the pot holder, turned to him shyly, as if she was a little girl that had got caught with her hand in the cookie jar. She wished it was a cookie jar.

"Is that what I think it is?" She scrunched up her face.

He smiled but didn't answer. He struck a match to light the centerpiece candles on the table stationed beside the warmth of the crackling fire in the fireplace. Then he pulled out her chair inviting her to dine.

"Dinner is served."

She felt as though she were in a restaurant kitchen at the chef's table for a special romantic private dining experience. A behind-the-scenes look at the culinary action without all the clatter of pots and pans. His music playlist added a language of love to the background. It was the best seat in the house tonight. If this wasn't a surefire way to create ambiance, she didn't know what was. She crossed her fingers in hope he wouldn't spoil the mood with clam chowder.

He ladled the soup into two bread bowls, and garnished it with crumbled bacon and chopped parsley. He served her and took the seat from across the table.

"This looks like clam chowder to me." She bit her lips. "We had a deal that you had to try my cheesy grits, then, and then only, I would sample your clam chowder."

He put both his elbows on the table, rested his chin on his hands and leaned in. "Firstly, I don't recall anyone stating the order of taste testing. Since you've been out of commission, grits will have to be served another day." He held his laughter. "Secondly, I don't remember a 'then and then only' protocol. If I'm not mistaken, you shook on it. A handshake is the same as a promise."

"I've been bamboozled! You tricked me. At the time I had no idea you cooked. From the looks of things, for all I know, you may be a professionally trained chef."

"I did tell you my mother is a chef."

"You just mentioned in passing that she was a sous-chef when you were young."

"So, you do listen." Gabe smiled. "I have a confession. My mom is not only a chef, she is a chef instructor at a culinary school in New Hampshire."

"That's fantastic! But just because she is a chef doesn't make you one. My dad is a woodcrafter and I can't cut a straight edge."

As he watched her squirm and verbalize her skepticism, he had to curb the urge to silence her with a kiss. Instead he played it safe and went with chowder.

He took his spoon and waved it in the air. "Do you want to be force fed?"

She lifted a tiny portion to her mouth.

Paused, held her nose with her free hand and downed the chowder in one gulp, then went for the wine.

He gawked at her with eyes wide open. "No, no. That won't do. That's cheating!"

"I didn't know there were rules," she retorted, gulping more wine.

From across the table, he leaned in, dipped his spoon in her bowl, and held it up to her mouth, teasing her like a child. "Young lady, if you don't eat this, you won't be getting any dessert."

Playing along, she asked, "What's for dessert?"

"Boston cream pie."

This time, she freely opened her mouth and let him feed her. With eyes half closed she slowly swept her tongue over her lips savoring the dish and his tender intimate gesture.

"That's surprisingly good!" She dabbed her lips with her napkin and gave him a self-indulgent look.

"I'm beginning to think you may be a spoiled brat!"

"I'll take that as a compliment."

The main course waited in the warming drawer of the oven. Gabe had prepared lobster.

"You'll love this lobster bake. It's lobster, corn, and red potatoes wrapped in foil, steamed over an open fire."

"I'm confused. One minute you're a professional chef, the next minute you're a chuck wagon pioneer cook."

"Close, but chuck wagon cooks use Dutch ovens, not aluminum foil," he schooled her. "But if you're interested, there's a great chuck wagon cooking school we could attend. I've always wanted to try it out. The overnight accommodations are in a Teepee."

"That sounds like every little boy's dream. I'd have to see pictures of the Teepee. I prefer luxury accommodations. How about glamping? Luxury digs and a gourmet campfire? I like the sound of that. You have the best of both worlds – couples and compromise."

"We can work up a business plan some other time. Let's enjoy this lobster bake while it's hot. This is one of my favorite meals. It's a little taste of New England in Tennessee." He was anxious for her opinion.

Seafood wasn't on her top-ten list of items to order off the menu, but she wasn't a novice either. She dipped the lobster in the lemon herb butter and took a bite.

"Delicious. You prepared it perfect. It's sweet. It always reminds me a little of shrimp, but it's chewier with a spongy texture."

He was impressed. He poured her another glass of wine. "The Riesling pairs well, it has sweet floral notes that bring out the natural sweetness of the lobster." He winked. "Don't gulp it this time."

She was impressed. "So, you're a gourmet chef and a wine connoisseur." She took another bite of the lobster. It was just a bite of protein to her, but it was a comfort food and memories for Gabe. She wanted to know more. She would add tonight's lobster bake to her memory list.

Enjoying herself, she took a sip of wine and questioned, what did she ever do to deserve the attention of this extraordinary man?

#

There's always a way to find out more information about your date. Shauna was guilty of running a DIY background check before a first date before. She never went as far as paying for an expensive exhaustive search. She didn't need to. She ruled social media and within a matter of minutes by searching Facebook, Instagram, Twitter, and Pinterest she had everything she needed to know to decide if there would be a first date. She'd surprised herself by not searching 'Gabriel Anderson'. Her family's stamp of approval was enough confirmation. Besides, she reminded herself, she was still on her social media detox plan. But in the short time since they'd met, she felt he knew more of her than she of him. She wanted to know more.

Comfortable in his company, she asked her date, "So, tell me more about your mother. You've had a close-up personal view of my family and I know very little of yours." They had moved from wine to coffee with their dessert. She drew the cup to her mouth, settling in for a nostalgic memoir.

Gabe felt comfortable enough to share his

story. "Mom joined her sorority sisters for a week-long spring break marathon of partying on the beach in Daytona her junior year of college. She met some guy the last night of the trip, had sex, and never saw him again."

She was surprised with the honest, blunt direction of the conversation. She tilted her head, rested her chin on the back of her hand and listened intently.

Gabe took a sip of his coffee and a bite of pie. "She only knew his first name. When I was old enough to understand, she told me I 'was conceived in lust, but born in love.' Raised Catholic, she didn't consider abortion. Her parents pushed for adoption."

"That must have been hard for you to grasp at a young age."

"I think it's hard to assimilate at any age, especially when you factor in emotion." He sat back comfortably in his chair. "Even though I was unplanned, there was never a moment I felt unwanted. I couldn't imagine a better mother."

"Did your grandparents honor her decision?" Shauna had only experienced strong family ties and found it hard to fathom family rejection.

"They withdrew financial support during her pregnancy, anticipating in hardship she would abdicate motherhood. It made her more determined. Her older sister, Alana, let her move in to her apartment in Boston. Mom accepted the lodging but no other monetary assistance. She found a restaurant who would hire her, worked full-time, and a local pregnancy care center assisted with diapers, formula, emotional support, and parenting classes. Aunt Alana was her birthing coach and my spare mother." Gabe took notice that Shauna's gaze never shifted focus, her soul-searching eyes stayed fully engaged. "Eventually, on my second birthday, my grandparents' hearts softened and they accepted us back in the family dynasty. Mom welcomed their love but not their loot."

Shauna's eyes stung. She batted her tears. Love and respect accented every word he spoke of his mother.

Gabe continued. "Mom is a big believer in reality living. She refused to believe the myth that her situation was hopeless and she was not capable of raising a child on her own. She said she accepted the situation and turned a nightmare into a dream come true. Motherhood was always an aspiration; it just became reality in an unconventional way."

"Do you see your mom often?"

"Not as often as I would like. We talk on the phone every few days." He paused his conversation for another sip of coffee that was getting cold. "Actually, Mom has shown interest in semi-retiring and possibly relocating to Spring Valley to help me expand our meal service. Currently, I only offer a gourmet breakfast for our guests. The updated kitchen is the first step to offering evening dining to our overnight guests and also to the public."

"Wow! What a great idea. You would have guaranteed reservations booked out for a year." An idea brightened her eyes. "She would become Spring Valley's own celebrity chef. She could even offer cooking classes, and—"

Gabe interrupted her. "You're great at marketing, I appreciate your excitement, but first, I need to convince her to move."

"I bet it won't take much convincing."

"I have Aunt Alana on my team, she's been dropping hints in their phone conversations. She misses her sister. Asheville is a short drive from here, compared to the ten-hour trip from New Hampshire." His mother preferred car trips to planes.

"I hope it works out for you. I'm sure you would love having her close."

"Close, yes. Working together would be a tightrope walk, but I think we can balance separate roles. Kitchens run according to a strict hierarchy. I've seen her in action; I definitely would have to relinquish anything that deals with dining to the head chef."

"Mom and Abby seem to be successfully running the shop together, especially considering Mom is a Christmas control freak." In a twirling motion of a finger near the temple she gestured the cuckoo sign. "If they can succeed and maintain a happy close mother-daughter relationship in the process, anyone can."

Since they were on the subject of mothers and he wanted to move on to a not-so-serious topic, Gabe added "I've got a mother question for you."

"I've just learned my mom has secrets of her own, so I may not be able to give you a truthful answer." Shauna almost wanted to gossip.

That piqued Gabe's interest, but he wanted to move on to a livelier conversation. "That sounds intriguing, but I want to know why Mrs. Christmas doesn't have a Christmas tree anywhere her house."

"Phew! That's an easy question." She smiled. "I was bracing for a doozy."

"I just found it odd that ornaments were on display throughout the house but not on a tree."

"We carry on an old Appalachian tradition in my family that can be traced back to the British Isles mountain settlers. They were mostly Scotch-Irish, who celebrated Old Christmas. Remember, I told you I was born on Old Christmas, January sixth?"

"I remember. Your name means 'present' in Celtic and you have special healing powers." He also thought she might be his divine gift this year. "My mom is from Irish descent. That makes me Boston Irish and you, Mountain Irish."

"You're correct about the meaning, however, I said it was folklore that babies born on January sixth have special healing powers. If I have powers, they haven't manifested." She touched her pink bandage and closed her eyes. "No, didn't work."

"Are you sure? You didn't say anything about having X-ray vision, just healing powers." He mirrored her healing gesture and touched his forehead with a concerning frown.

"I'm sure. It still hurts like the dickens. Anyways, in our family we put up a freshly cut tree and decorate it on Christmas Eve. Santa fills the stocking hung on the chimney and places twelve gifts under the tree for each family member."

"That's a lot of presents under a tree."

"It is, but most are small gifts. We open our stocking stuffers on Christmas morning, then each following day after Christmas, until January six, we open one of the gifts. On the sixth we take down the tree."

"I bet the twins love that tradition. It's a never-ending celebration."

"Mom and Daddy love it, too. They get a visit from their grandkids twelve straight days in a row."

"The Catholic church observes January sixth as the Feast of the Epiphany, the showing forth of God; honoring the visit of the Magi's visit to the infant Jesus."

"Exactly! Same tradition, different name." With a laugh, she leaned back in the chair to stretch her sore muscles and instinctively pulled her hair up and wound it around her head, as if to wrap it in a bun. After the stretch she dropped the locks to fall loosely back to her shoulder and trickle down her back. She looked peaceful, content, and drive-him-crazy sensuous. But he made no advance toward her.

It wasn't from the lack of desire, he wanted to wrap her in his arms and drown in her love. He was ready. He was more than ready. But the words her father had spoken held him back. Only hours before, when Ryan personally delivered and installed the fireplace mantle, before he left the inn, he shook Gabe's hand and said, "I see the way you look at Shauna. Don't give up. She just needs time."

Gabe was not planning on giving up. He just hoped it didn't take too long. When Shauna arrived for the holidays in Spring Valley, hope came to town. His hope.

Chapter Twenty-One

She was still on the mend. Shauna needed all the energy she could muster to pull her thoughts together and finalize plans for the ACHIEVE Christmas wish. There were a dozen moms and their children counting on it. Come rain, shine, hell or high water she was determined not to let them down.

She'd had a restless night. When she'd closed her eyes the image of Gabe sitting across from her, relaxed, engaged in conversation, lingered in her head. Images resided all night. Standing at the counter with a chef knife at work, looking like a pro; smiling and welcoming her to his abode. From across the table, leaning in, dipping his spoon in her bowl, holding it up to her mouth, teasing her like a child, feeding her his near perfect food as she savored the dish and his tender intimate gesture.

He listened. He inquired. He shared. He understood. He teased. He comforted. He reminisced. He dreamed. He was a man of many facets, all of them pleasing.

She had to push those dreamy thoughts aside and get back to the task for the morning – finalizing the evening's Christmas cookie baking activity. Abiding by the rules of recruiting volunteers for the project, she invited Abby and her family to join Gabe and her at the inn. They would bake the cookies, and prepare them for the kids to decorate at the party. It was a great idea. They could kill two birds with one stone. Decoration craft and dessert.

She frowned at the idiom that slipped in to her thoughts. She'd heard those words all of her life and let them slip out on occasion. Her politically correct friends in Atlanta would have been quick to give her the evil eye. She decided to delete that particular lingo from her data bank.

She wasn't up to in-person shopping, so she ordered all the items on the shopping list from the grocer through their online app. Gabe volunteered to curbside pick-up and she would prepare the kitchen before everyone arrived.

#

Joyful. That's how Shauna felt as she went about the kitchen gathering the must-have baking tools for their cookie bake. As she roamed from cabinet to cabinet, drawer to drawer, she was impressed with the kitchen gadgets and gizmos Gabe had stocked in his kitchen. Martha Stewart would feel right at home.

It was the season of giving and she felt great joy in helping others. Her gran whispered in her heart, "*Tidings of comfort and joy.*" She burst into song, completing the lyrics to, 'God Rest Ye Merry Gentlemen'. She didn't need her iPhone to search for the lyrics, she knew them by heart. She knew all the carols by heart. Her mom was responsible for that musical feat. "*God rest ye merry gentlemen, let nothing you dismay, remember Christ our Savior was born on Christmas Day...*"

Her back to the door and with her bellowing voice, she didn't realize she wasn't alone. He watched her dancing around and singing about the kitchen. "I didn't know you could sing." Smiling, paying her a compliment, he said, "You could go on the road."

Startled, a wooden mixing spoon flew out of her hand. She was relieved when she realized it was Gabe, she laughed and swatted at him. "You scared me. What are you doing sneaking in?" Her heart beat fast.

Amused by the flying utensil and surprised by the question, he sat the grocery bags on the counter, and held her by the shoulders with both hands. Pretending she was concussed with amnesia, he calmly spoke in slow motion, "I'm Gabe Anderson. I am not sneaking in. I live here." He tilted his head and glanced up and down for further examination.

"Stop it!" This time she used a dish towel to whack him and halt the teasing. "I'm well aware of who you are and who I am." Her heart still raced. She had to admit, that was funny.

He let her go and started to unload the grocery bags. "I'm glad you ordered online and left the shopping to the professionals." He piled items on the counter. "Baking is not my forte, it would have taken me forever. We would have been exchanging texts to confirm if I had the correct ingredients in the cart."

"I'm sure you would have managed." She started rummaging through the ingredients, checking them off her list item by item and organizing them on the counter. "I have fun cooking with the twins, but I've found it best to have everything ready and waiting. Their favorite part is cracking eggs and mixing. So beware, it will get chaotic and messy – really messy."

"I'll create their own cooking stations. You and Abby team up with Paige, and Tyler and I will team up with Bryce."

"There you go, sounding like a professional chef again." She sent him a quick smile of approval.

He opened a large shopping bag stowed in the pantry and pulled out matching holiday aprons in adult and kid sizes he'd purchased earlier that day at a local cooking store. "We can have a Christmas Cookie Challenge, boys against the girls." Without asking, he slipped an apron's loop over her head, and tied the back strings around her waist. "Perfect, now you look like a professional!" He tied his on.

"What a fun idea! I'm guessing somebody

has been watching the Food Network in his spare time." She also guessed that he would be a great dad, someday.

He was a magician and pulled more items out of the bag.

"I couldn't resist." He held up a kid-size tall, round, white chef hat. "Don't worry I didn't buy any for the adults."

"You are amazing! Cooking in the inn's kitchen, the chef costume, a cookie bakeoff; they will pester their parents to open their own restaurant!"

"That would be cool! There used to be a restaurant in New York, Twins Restaurant on the Upper East Side that was owned by twins and it was staffed by identical twins."

"Now, that's crazy!" She imagined staffing would have been a nightmare.

"This will be a good test-kitchen. We need to think easy, kid-friendly, since we'll have preschoolers decorating the cookies at the party. If it's a challenge for Paige and Bryce, we'll need to adjust."

"Yes, chef." She surrendered to the chain of command.

He gave her that irresistible smile and raised his eyebrows. "I knew I should have given into temptation and purchased the 'Kiss the Cook' apron."

"Yes, chef." Up until now, she had managed to control her impulses. But now she went with the impulse and latched on to his apron, pulled him to her lips and gave him a passionate kiss. He surrendered.

The badly timed, intrusive knock on the back door interrupted their moment. Their heart-jolting moment. Gabe reluctantly broke away to answer the door, but quickly returned for another touch of her lips. They could wait. He couldn't.

"Knock, knock, anybody home?" Since they were expected, Abby didn't wait for someone to open the door. She stepped in. She saw. She stopped. Her little family piled up behind her like dominos falling. "Are we interrupting?" Her eyes danced with delight. This was unexpected. This was exactly what she had hoped for her sister. "We can take the kids for cocoa and return later."

Astonished, awakened, and submerged in her kiss, Gabe didn't want to move. She had thrown him a curve. Up until now, he had initiated any physical affection. He wasn't complaining, he was more than pleased. But he knew he had to move or motion Abby to leave. Gabe turned to greet his guests.

Off balanced, and a little embarrassed by her forwardness, Shauna could feel her face flush and quickly made a makeshift fan from a recipe card. "Whew! It's hot in here."

Abby thought it sweet and comical, Shauna was not the actor in the family – she held that title. Abby winked at her little sis, and unbundled the kids, giving Shauna ample time for the red in her cheeks to subside.

"Gabe, are you going to offer your guest a glass of wine?" Abby assigned Gabe an errand, allowing him time to recoup as well. She was excellent at family management strategies.

Tyler, oblivious to the scene they'd walked in on, reminded Gabe on his way to the wine rack, "When you mix these two sisters with bubbly, look out!"

Shauna decided she didn't need any wine; her face was flushed and her head was already spinning.

Gabe tried not to dwell on Shauna. It was difficult. No, it was impossible. Unsolicited, she just lovingly kissed him in his kitchen. He cleared his head, as much as humanly possible, and went about the task at hand. He surprised the twins with their special aprons and chef hats.

His surprise trumped theirs. Their eyes almost popped out of their heads. Their ginger curls bounced as they squealed in delight when they saw the cute gingerbread man on the front of the apron with a white chef hat that matched theirs. Gabe decided it had been a wise call to book an overnight stay for Big Papi in Camp Ruff-N-More kennel. Add him in the kitchen mix and mayhem would have conquered; leaving a havoc-wreaked disaster in its wake.

Everyone in town knew the twins and adored their bubbling personalities. As brother-sister fraternal twins they were not identical, but looked enough alike that you knew they were siblings. The ginger curls, rosy cheeks, and those rare blue eyes. Abby made contrasting fashion choices for the kids, hoping they would have their own unique style. Their individual personalities seemed to balance one another. Abby was a pro at mothering the twins. She already knew the good, bad, and ugly, and how to address the issues. They were fascinating and baffling. One minute they would be giggling and playing, the next they would be pulling hair. Abby seemed to take it in her stride.

Nothing reminded Abby more of their childhood than Christmas sugar cookies. She was the best baker in their clan and self-appointed Keeper-of-the-Family-Recipe-Box. She cherished that vintage wood box and the secrets it held as if it were gold plated. The simple, pine, hand-carved treasure had been passed down in the Murphy family from generation to generation. It guarded the sugar cookie recipe that brought back precious memories of Abby and Shauna, standing on kitchen chairs to reach the counter, rolling out the dough and cutting the shapes with their mother and grandmother.

The bakers were set in their cooking stations, ready for the competition to start. Gabe would have been the envy of the Bristol Motor Speedway announcer. "Chefs, start your mixers!" He held a rolling pin high in the air and quickly lowered it to his side. Special effects cued, a loud whirr from the blenders filled the air.

Rockin' to the holiday music cranked up in the background, they measured, cracked, mixed, stirred, and frosted their way through the evening. Occasional giggling fits broke out amongst the kids and adults alike. When the Cookie Challenge winners were declared, with all the exuberant woohoos, yippees, and celebration dancing, you would have thought the guys had won the NASCAR All-Star Race. Tyler and Gabe hoisted Bryce on their shoulders for a final victory lap. The only thing missing was the champagne spraying. The girls wanted to douse them with cold water. Abby and Tyler managed parenthood like old pros, all the while, making memories.

Gabe and Shauna were making memories of their own. They had a hard time keeping their eyes off each other from their separate cooking stations. Stolen glances. Easy smiles. Flirtation eyes. With that one impulse, she removed the doubt. Tonight, he knew how she felt.

The kitchen smelled of vanilla and almond – it smelled like Christmas. Gabe thought love was in the air.

Chapter Twenty-Two

From the looks of things outside Shauna's window, a significant weather event was taking place. A white Christmas was not the norm in East Tennessee. Shauna could count on one hand when they'd had more than a few inches of snow fall before the twenty-fifth. One of the worst blizzards in history was the year her gran encountered one of God's invisible hosts, when the angel appeared and led her to safety. Another memory was the magical Narnia winter snowfall at her grandparents' cabin and their sister-search for Father Christmas.

The day before, Shauna joined her family for Sunday church services. Her mom and Abby opened the store at noon and left the rest of the family to fend for themselves. She had lunch with her daddy, the twins, and Tyler, then spent the rest of the afternoon relaxing on the couch with her comfort cat and a cozy Christmas romance novel. She and Gabe exchanged flirty texts. Her favorites he sent were, *You've kept me smiling all day* and *I have so much to do, but I keep getting distracted thinking about you.* She lifted her self-imposed social media detox moratorium. The hiatus was a healthy break when she felt anxiety, vulnerability, and stress. It was an easy way to set boundaries. She felt stronger. At one time she dreaded opening a text. Now, she welcomed them.

It had snowed through the night, followed by a wintry mix throughout the early morning. When they scheduled the Christmas party for ACHIEVE, this was not showing in the extended forecast on her trusty weather app. It only predicted flurries. She smiled thinking of Mr. Barnett sitting in his rocker, reading the Farmer's Almanac, forewarning her of the predicted heavy snowfall. Technology lost the battle in this case. She should have trusted the Farmer's Almanac. After all, she knew they've been predicting the weather longer than the National Weather Service. Like Mr. Barnett, her gran had been a true believer.

She looked out the window and hoped the snow plows that rumbled down Main Street would forge a path for Santa's arrival at the Train Depot. She and Gabe had promised them a magical evening. She didn't want to break their promise and the kids' little hearts.

Gabe pulled his rental SUV into her driveway as easy as a snowmobile. She met him at the door as he trudged through the wet snow. He stopped a few feet from the porch admiring the blanket of snow. "I'm loving this four-wheel drive and this snow. This morning while I shoveled the sidewalk, I felt like I was back home in New Hampshire getting slammed by a wicked nor'easter. As soon as I cleared a path, it covered over. I couldn't keep up with the accumulation, so I gave up." His aching shoulders reminded him that he shouldn't have even attempted the task.

She motioned for him to come in, out of the cold. "I'm not loving this snow. I hate it! I can't believe it."

He wanted to drag her out in the snow, but she was still recovering. When he stepped on the porch he reached for her arm pretending. "Come on, you're an angel, let's make snow angels."

She pulled back. "Don't you dare!" She laughed and then commanded, "Get in here!"

He willingly complied. "So, you're like Big Papi, he didn't want to put his paw in the cold snow this morning, even when he begged at the door for his potty break. He's become a pampered pooch."

"Haven't we all?" She grabbed his arm as he stomped the snow from his boots. Before he could unzip his coat, she wrapped her arms around his neck and kissed him.

Surprised, he responded, "Well, good morning to you," and met her lips once more.

Comfortable in his arms, she stayed and voiced her concerns. "I'm worried about tonight." Chin lifted, with her eyes still on his lips, she pouted.

He studied her. A grin emerged. She wore a

comfy wooly turtleneck, slim fit jeans and fuzzy holiday cat socks. Her curly locks were pulled up in that pineapple top knot. He hadn't seen her hair in this style. He liked it. It made him think of those curly bows stuck on top of Christmas packages. She was his perfect, unexpected present.

He tried to relieve her worries. "The road crew is clearing all the main thoroughfares and the weather woman on the local news calls for sun and warmer temperatures by noon."

Her mood altered, more in line with her natural curly-q-bow on top of her head. "Great! Maybe we can pull this party off, after all."

Maybe he gave her the wrong impression. He didn't want to raise her anxiety but they had to live in reality. "We can't do anything about the weather. It's out of our control. We may just have to reschedule the party." Disappointment showed on her face. "Let's just watch, wait, and see. We have a few hours before we have to decide."

She was still in his arms melting his heart as snow on his boots melted into a puddle on the floor. "I don't want to let you go, but I've got to take these boots off and wipe up this floor, before it floods."

She sighed and went to the bathroom to retrieve a towel.

"We just have to double-check the weather to make sure everyone has safe transportation. If the temperatures climb the snow will melt, but if they fall, we'll have to deal with black ice." Both of their minds veered to their recent car accident.

"That's for sure!" she agreed.

"Where's your clicker? Let's watch the weather."

She loved the way he dropped his R's. "My clicker? Are you referring to the remote control?"

"Yes, the clicker." He smiled and settled that. She tossed him the remote.

A motion on the back deck distracted her. She looked out and saw her little friend. It was hard to miss the brilliant-red bird against the winter backdrop of the white snow piled on the railing. He was her heaven-sent messenger – this was a good sign.

#

The party was cancelled. The sun showed up by noon. It melted the snow almost as fast as it fell, but the forecast called for freezing temperatures in the afternoon. They decided it was too risky for young moms to be out driving on the roads on a night like this.

"We need to make it official and call everyone to let them know we've cancelled." Gabe scrolled through his phone searching for contact numbers.

"Wait, just give me a minute to think." Shauna wasn't about to give up. She had a reputation as the best social media problem solver. Surely, she thought, she could solve this dilemma. Strategies bounced around in her head as she sat on the couch, snuggled up to Gabe. Suddenly, she sat straight up and turned to face him. Her sapphire eyes danced with excitement. "I know Santa!"

Confused, Gabe cocked his head. "Yes, we've already established that fact. You're close enough that your dad is building his coffin." He teased with that smile.

She grabbed a fluffy holiday pillow and in fun hit him on the head. In a flash, he found the matching pillow that was tucked behind him and drew his arm back, ready for battle. "I give you fair warning, I will win this pillow fight."

She froze in motion, ready for the second strike but mulled over her decision. She was up for a cozy combat but not an all-out war. With his physique, for all she knew, he could be in a fight club. She threw her arms up in surrender and called a truce before the battle even began. "I challenge you at a later date. We don't have time for this, now."

She switched gears and went into Santa mode.

"We didn't have a contingency plan, but I do now. Santa has a big red truck that could plow through any snow on the back roads. With only twelve families we can arrange a personal delivery from Santa. We could have him snap a quick selfie, then on to the next house."

"You're a beautiful genius." He held her face with both hands and congratulated her with a kiss.

"It will be our Christmas party-in-a-box. Here's what we can do. You already have everything for the party organized at the inn that we were going to transfer to the Train Depot. Mom has tons of extra-large holiday storage boxes we could use for each family. They are factory decorated; they won't need to be wrapped. Here's what we're going to do. If we hurry, at one we can be at the inn and fill the boxes with the individual gifts, the fruit and candy bag, the craft, and the cookies. We have enough decorating icing tubes we can include one in each box and the kids can decorate their cookies at home."

"I'll order more pizzas so each family has their own. I'll pay for the extra pies." He raised his hand before she could utter the words. "Don't waste your breath with your follow-the-rules speech. This is a special circumstance. I'm doing it."

"Testy, are we?" She raised an eyebrow and smiled. "We already have the names of the kids, now we need their addresses. I'll call Mrs. Bowman and see if she will provide those ASAP. And I'll ask her to have the families that live out in the rural area to tie a ribbon around the mail box."

He gave her an inquisitive look.

She explained, "We won't be able to rely on GPS, there's spotty coverage in the foothills where the mountains block the signal."

"Good idea. That's happened to me a few times on hikes."

She closed her eyes, willing any forgotten items to surface and sat silent for a moment. "Santa! I've got to call and see if he can start delivering by two or three this afternoon. We can follow in the SUV and be his elves." That idea garnished a big smile.

"Whoa, don't even think it! I am not wearing an elf costume." He spoke it slow and loudly, so there was no misunderstanding.

"I'm sure Mrs. Christmas has one stored somewhere. I vaguely remember from that college summer trip I took with Abby and Tyler, and that ruggedly handsome white-water rafting guy in his wetsuit at the helm of the raft." She did a quick double raise of her eyebrows. "You looked good! You would also look good in green elf tights. Are you sure?" She lied, it wasn't a vague memory, his image from long ago was forever etched in her mind.

"Positive! I'm not wearing green tights!" He was also positive she hadn't mentioned she remembered him that summer. She had been thinking of him a lot longer than he knew.

"Depending on how many live out on the backroads, Santa will need plenty of time to deliver before the kids' bedtimes." Shauna calculated the time.

"Santa's coming early this year!" Shauna exclaimed.

Chapter Twenty-Three

By three, the party-in-a-box mission was complete and loaded in Santa's truck. Mrs. Bowman, the woman who made the Ornament of Hope wish, asked if she could join in the fun. She dressed as Mrs. Claus and sat in the front seat with her pretend husband, excited to make this magical trip. Gabe and Shauna joined the yuletide caravan in their vehicle, loaded up with pizzas.

Prepared for snow in higher elevations, Santa had tire chains, and Gabe threw in a snow shovel if they needed to shovel a path to a porch. The Red Survival Backpack, he placed in the back seat, caused Shauna concern.

\#

So far, so good. The party-in-a-box was a hit! Santa was welcomed with open arms and squeals of delight. Shauna would have loved to watch the kids dig in and discover their toys and goodies, but after selfies with Santa and Mrs. Claus, they had to be on their merry way delivering packages to more boys and girls. She hoped they had created a lasting memory for the little ones. She knew her memory would last a lifetime.

Shauna's anxieties did not go unnoticed. In the beginning, the excitement of their adventure tamped down the terror she felt of driving in bad road conditions. It was obvious that terror had been released. Gabe couldn't help but notice that she gasped at the slightest skid, her knuckles turned white from tightly clutching the grab handle on the door, and her left leg nervously bounced up and down in rapid movement like a scared little bunny.

"I have a suggestion," he proceeded with cautious concern. "After this last stop in town, why don't I drop you off at the cottage and I'll make the out-in-the-country trips solo?" He added playfully, "I'll still be in the Santa caravan, so you don't have to worry, the big guy in the red suit will keep me safe."

She let out a big sigh. "Whew! I think you may be right. As my gran used to say, I'm as nervous as a cat on a hot tin roof." She didn't tell him about the shortness of breath, heart palpitations, and hot flashes. Still clutching the grab handle, she took him up on his offer.

Since Santa was watching and she wanted to stay off the naughty list, she leaned over and gave Gabe a quick peck on the cheek and made him promise to text her as soon as he returned to the inn. She walked to the cottage, turned, and waved as they drove away.

Her dad saw the headlights in the driveway.

Thinking there was no way they could have delivered all of the packages in that amount of time, he called Shauna on her cell phone to get an update.

"Hi baby girl, is everything alright?"

"I'm fine, Daddy. I was just getting a little tired and thought it best to call it a night early. Gabe has everything under control." She wasn't being totally honest with her daddy, she didn't want to alarm him, but after their little adventure, she was feeling a bit out of control. She needed to rest and settle her nerves.

"How did it go, so far? I bet the kids loved it."

"They did, especially the visit from Santa and Mrs. Claus. You do know that you have the coolest best friend in the world, don't you?"

"Did you say Mrs. Claus? He must have a secret he's not shared. You do know he's still single."

She couldn't help but giggle. "Don't worry, it was the lady who made the wish, she really wanted to be a part of the delivery, so she came up with the idea. They looked kind of cute together. She's a divorcee, too, so maybe there will be a little Christmas magic and you'll be his best man before you know it."

"I'm glad it worked out, so he could join in granting the wish tonight. He's a great guy and would do anything for our family."

"Thanks for checking in on me, Daddy. Give Mom a hug and kiss. I'm going to scrounge up something to nibble on and go to bed early. Love you."

"Love you." The call ended. Something told him he should be concerned. He prayed for his daughter.

#

The last delivery was the most difficult. They saw the big red ribbon tied on the mailbox, signaling it was the correct address. They drove down an unpaved bumpy road, praying they wouldn't get stuck in the mud and snow. The scene was familiar. Gabe had driven past small modest homes and mobile homes, tucked back in a hollow, dozens of times on his way to a mountain hike. He often pictured in his mind's eye who might live in those dwellings, solely based on the media's negative stereotypes of people of Appalachia. Tonight, he would stop. Tonight, he would knock on a door. Tonight, he would face reality living.

The warm glow of the porch light lit the path to the front door. Thanks to Santa, the greetings were never awkward. Chaos commenced. The pizza box flew open as soon as it hit the coffee table. They didn't seem to mind the cold pizza. The three kids twirled around, dancing in excitement, chomping on their dinner as Santa got comfy in a lazy boy chair. The house smelled of pine from the newly cut and decorated tree that sat in front of the window. The lights all over the tree were bright enough to light up an entire room.

Their party-in-a-box had two gifts for the

children. Gabe's heart sank when he saw three children and asked if they had made a mistake.

"No." She turned her back, so the kids couldn't hear her and talked in a soft tone. "My sister is having a rough time, she's in the hospital from an overdose. I'm keeping my nephew with us until she can get some help and get cleaned up." While she chatted, the kids gathered around their famous guests.

Gabe presented an understanding nod, even though he didn't have a clue of what she or her sister faced. That wasn't his world. He had only seen the staggering death count of opioid-involved overdoses splashed in the headlines, and announcements of new initiatives focused on finding solutions to this deadly onslaught of opioids in the Appalachian region. Tonight, he came face to face with the ripple effect – the impact of the epidemic on families. That statistic wasn't just a headline on a newsfeed – it was real. He was sitting on Santa's lap. Gabe wondered what the little boy wished when he whispered in Santa's ear.

#

"I think I have something perfect for him. I'll be right back." As he stepped out on the porch, before he shut out the cold, he turned to ask the boy's name, so he could write it on the gift tag.

She answered, "His name is Gabriel. Just like the angel."

He almost tumbled off the porch and down the steps. God wasn't whispering prompts, tonight – he was shouting. Gabe ran to the Jeep to retrieve a gift he had purchased, and stowed in the back seat, just in case they needed an extra present. It was a baseball glove and ball. The same as his prized childhood baseball glove, the only gift his mother could manage to place under the tree when he was six years old. This little guy appeared to be about the same age.

Gabe whispered a prayer, "Bless this little boy, Gabriel, like you've blessed me." He hurried back inside with the wrapped memory, and placed it under the tree.

The woman gave him one of those awkward, I-hug-everybody-hugs to thank him. "You'll never know how much this means to me and my family." Tears that lived always close to the surface coursed down her face in a mixture of joy and sadness.

Observing the interaction, Mrs. Claus walked over and wrapped her in a big grandmotherly hug, to help her conceal the sobs she usually hid from the kids. After a few seconds, she dried her tears and gathered the family for selfies with Santa, Mrs. Claus, and Gabe. They bid their farewells with a Ho! Ho! Ho! and started the bumpy ride back to Spring Valley.

On the lonely, dark drive home he reflected on the night's mission of hope. He wished Shauna was sitting in the bucket seat beside him. He thought of the night that launched these assignments when, together, they chose their ornaments from the Giving Tree, and when Ada read the scripture from Isaiah. Ada said they would *glow in the darkness* in our quest to fulfill these Christmas wishes. He didn't know her words would prove to be so literal. The acts of kindness brought a glow to their faces and to their homes.

He was inspired by the young single moms he met, who struggled to beat the odds and chose to fight and overcome poverty through higher education. Fighting to protect their children and provide a brighter future. Fighting against the myth that they can't improve themselves without leaving the mountains and people they love.

Tonight changed him. He saw his mother's reflection in their eyes. The struggles his mother faced in New England, thirty years ago, were similar struggles these moms in Appalachia faced today. The common thread that binds them is love for their children. The powerful force that will carry them through their journey of hope. He was living proof.

#

It was late when he texted.

I'm back at the inn. Good night.

Shauna didn't respond. He assumed she was sound asleep.

Chapter Twenty-Four

The late-night call stunned him. His mother's conversation was totally unexpected. He needed to process. He needed to contemplate. He knew where he needed to go. He heard the mountains calling.

Before daybreak he found himself driving toward his favorite highlands. He needed his quiet place. To think. To pray. To decide. He felt close to God in the mountains. His favored psalm came to mind, *I lift my eyes to the mountains, where does my help come from? My help comes from the Lord.* He answered the mountain's call.

The severe weather band moved east. The main roads cleared. If needed, the four-wheel-drive system would power him through snow in higher elevations. Big Papi gave him those big, sad puppy-dog eyes when he was left behind at the inn. Gabe didn't need any distractions.

Just as the sunrise cast a golden glow over the rolling mountains, he parked the Jeep in a clearing, hitched on his hiking daypack, pulled on his gloves, and grabbed his trekking poles.

Frozen trail crunched under his boots as he hiked up the steep embankment. The cold air bit him in the lungs as he puffed hard breaths, swirling and scattering in the air. He wasn't at 100 percent. He questioned his stamina, and was glad he had trekking poles in hand for the steady climb. He stopped for a moment to catch his breath and pulled his wool beanie down further to shield his ears. He climbed on. Light streamed through the trees in the fir forest, reflecting sparkles on the meandering snow path that led him to the mountaintop – his quiet place. He unhitched his daypack. His waterproof snow pants kept him dry as he sat on the ground and pulled out a bottle of water to hydrate. He strapped on his binoculars to view two white-tailed deer emerging from the thick of the forest. He assumed they were about their morning habit during the frosty winter months, foraging on acorns and rhododendron plants. They walked along the shore of Lady Lake in search of shallow spot to quench their thirst. The psalm came to his mind, *As the deer longs for streams of water, so I long for you, O God.* He prayed. Then, he contemplated.

His mom had decided she didn't want to work for him, instead, she and Aunt Alana wanted to buy the inn. Not manage. *Own*. She was so excited, trying to convince him the idea was genius. Alana's years of experience from working at the Biltmore Inn, combined with her expertise as a chef, were the perfect ingredients for a recipe for success. A small inn, a small town, a big adventure for two sisters in semi-retirement. She tried closing the deal with the idea it would free him up to pursue his own interests and, if he wanted, he would have time to fulfill his lifelong dream – hike the entire AT.

It came with a hitch. There's always a hitch. They were ready to make the move now, if he was ready to let go. He had to decide.

Dreams change. People change. He sat on the very land he dreamed of someday building a cabin and the base for an all-inclusive outdoor adventure tour company. He envisioned specializing in trail hiking, fly fishing in the river, water rafting, kayaking on the lake, winter backcountry skiing, anything outdoors. He would even offer glamping.

After Robin's death, he considered selling the inn and venturing out. He wrestled with the betraying thoughts and resolved to remain innkeeping; he couldn't abandon Robin's legacy. Times changed. His thoughts evolved. He knew she had loved her mother-in-law and Aunt Alana, who were much more suited than Gabe to carry on her vision and legacy for the inn. Robin wouldn't feel betrayed. She would be proud.

He could no longer live in the past. He considered the future. Gabe prayed. *Give me strength, Lord, give me wisdom*.

A high-pitched whistling sound echoed in the mountains and invaded his thoughts. He lifted his binoculars to his eyes and rose for a full view.

He spotted a glorious bald eagle swoop down across the lake. Its wings grazed the water, then it soared back to the sky, as if delivering a message from the Creator. *Those who hope in the Lord will renew their strength. They will soar on wings like eagles; they will run and not grow weary; they will walk and not be faint.*

Gabe whispered, "Thank you, Lord. You never fail. You are my strength."

Inspired, he sat again. The view was spectacular. The fog that spent the evening resting in the mountains' valleys, carried a wisp of mist that lazily weaved in and out of the hollows, dawdled between the basins of the hills, and drifted low over the lake, deliberately trying to escape the burn of morning sunrays. Gabe smiled, thinking it would be a perfect landscape for a Bob Ross masterpiece.

He'd hosted a Bob Ross-style workshop at the inn with a local artist. Gabe wasn't much of a painter, but there was something hypnotic about Bob's smooth voice. He admitted, to the attendees at the workshop, that during a season of insomnia, night after night, he would find the clicker to turn on the TV and watch the *Joy of Painting* to lull him to sleep. He and Bob were kindred spirits in their love for the main subject – the almighty mountains. Bob spoke of each element in his art, as if describing friends. He would paint a single happy tree, decide it looked too lonely, then add a happy little tree friend. Happy little clouds, filled a happy sky, over a charming little cabin. Bob seemed to be a happy little man.

Gabe recalled the most interesting Bob Ross trivia the instructor shared. Out of all his works of art, people were only included twice in his paintings. Once, there was a silhouette of a man at a campfire. The other painting included two people walking in the woods. Gabe stopped himself in mid-thought. That's it!

The fog lifted from Gabe's brain. Everything was clear. He had his answer. That's all he needed; a cabin, a campfire, and Shauna.

He'd had a mountaintop experience. He wanted to tell Shauna. His cell only had one bar. He tried, anyway. It went straight to voice mail. He wanted to explain everything, but not in a voice mail. He decided to leave a short message.

I have a buyer for the inn. We need to talk.

He ended the call.

\#

Just when Shauna thought her emotions were back on solid ground, PTSD struck and sent emotional shockwaves, that shook her to the core. She'd underestimated the effects of the recent trauma from the car accident. She'd underestimated how her mind would react as she rode in a vehicle in similar conditions as the night of the collision. She'd underestimated a lot of things. Vivid nightmares returned. The evildoer reappeared for a haunting visit. He entered her dreams and escorted her back to the toxic work environment where the sexual harassment began. He took her to his private office, where he closed the door, removed his clothes and made unwanted sexual advances toward her. He took her to the dark shadowed corner of a parking lot where he sat outside her apartment, and watched and waited. He transported her back to the scene of the accident. But in her dream, the car accident wasn't with Gabe, she was alone, injured, trying to escape her stalker. The only deliverance from the nightmare was to wake. She woke up shaking, shouting, and her heart racing.

The recurring dream had a new figure. As her evildoer lay in wait in the veil of darkness outside her apartment, a vicious lion with red devil eyes stood at his right side. Staring. Stalking. It was evil personified. Shauna consciously controlled her breathing to calm her nerves. Long, slow breaths in through her nose. Count to three. Exhale slowly through pursed lips. Repeat. She breathed herself calm. She prayed. She prayed a psalm she read earlier that morning, *Hide me in the shadow of your wing from the wicked who are out to destroy me, they are like a lion, hungry for prey.* She sobbed. She fell back to sleep on a tear-soaked pillow.

When Gabe's early-morning call came, she wasn't in the right mind to talk, and sent it straight to voice mail. She listened. The cryptic voice message was just about enough to push her over the edge. She had fallen asleep on the couch and didn't hear the chime when he'd texted last night. It was a far cry from the flirty texts they had exchanged. Just a short, send-to-a-stranger kind of text. *I'm back at the inn. Good night.* She thought maybe her panicky get-me-out-of-this-car-before-I-have-a nervous-breakdown behavior may have scared him off.

He said he was trying to tamp down his Northerner bluntness, but how else was she supposed to interpret the text and his voice message except for being rude? Or was he wanting a way out. Plus, since when did he have a buyer for the inn? He didn't even have it on the market.

She sipped on her coffee and thought through it with a mixture of frustration and apathy. The inn brought Gabe to Spring Valley. She understood his dilemma. The inn was a part of his past – Robin's legacy. Shauna had no connection to the inn, except for Gabe. Would he just choose to up and sell and move from Spring Valley on a moment's notice?

She needed to process her thoughts. She never spoke of her post-traumatic stress disorder diagnosis to her family, or to anyone else for that matter. She thought it was a little over the top, thinking the diagnosis of PTSD was reserved for soldiers. Her therapist assured her it effects a broad range of people, not just soldiers. Five out of every ten women experience a traumatic event. Shauna could never have imagined she would be one of those five. But she was. There were times when she questioned her decision to expose her abuser. She could have just hidden the secret in a dark closet. Her therapist applauded her decision to expose the destructive act for what it truly was – evil. She explained to Shauna that healing happens when darkness is exposed to light. Her Gran whispered, *Walk in God's pure light; there's no darkness in him.*

Shauna closed her eyes to quiet her thoughts so she could invoke her therapist's counsel. She visualized sitting in the office listening to her voice: *It will be a long journey to recovery... You will have setbacks... A traumatic event may retraumatize you... Connect with family and friends... Use talk therapy to work out your feelings.*

She opened her eyes and reached for her phone. Talk therapy. That's exactly what I need!

"Abby."

"Shauna, you sound distraught. Are you okay?" Abby's mind went in a million different directions.

Shauna couldn't even muster up the energy to conceal her melancholy behind the mask of smiling depression. It became second nature for quite some time. She would mask her depression behind smiles, laughter, and a cheery voice. Recently, she took it off and set the mask aside. She needed to leave it there.

"I know you're at work, but could Tyler manage the twins tonight, so you can come over for a sister slumber party? I need talk therapy. I really need it bad."

"That's not a problem, we can work it out." Abby was already organizing her plans in her mind as she spoke. "I'll bring your favorite Chinese carry-out and plenty of snacks."

Shauna couldn't even think about food, but she knew Abby couldn't think without it, so she didn't bother to say her stomach was in knots.

"I'll be there by six. Are you sure you'll be okay until then?" Mother-hen Abby had to make certain. She was worried.

"I'll be fine. See you tonight. Love you, sis. Thank you."

"Love you." She reassured her, "If you need anything before then, just call or text. Promise me." Abby used to make her pinky promise when she was little.

"I promise."

Shauna broke her promise before the call ended. She needed her now.

There was a knock on the door.

Chapter Twenty-Five

The road snaked down the mountain, twisting and turning from one hairpin turn to the next. Gabe wanted to hurry and get to Shauna to share his mountaintop experience and plans for his future – their future – but the slick surface of the road forced him to slow down and soak up the wintry scene. The north-facing slope remained shaded throughout most of the day, filtering out the sunlight's attempt to melt the snow blanket. The fir trees heavy with sparkly snow, branches almost touching the ground, appeared as if they bowed to their Maker. He enjoyed the winter hikes in Tennessee, but the snow hikes in New Hampshire, took on a whole different dimension in the White Mountains. A winter 'Hike in the Whites' meant trekking through several feet of snow, wicked wind, and below freezing temperatures. He loved every minute of it.

His tenth Christmas, his mom surprised him with his only wish – a winter camping trip. That was the night the mountains grabbed his heart and wouldn't let go. He became mountain obsessed. He smiled thinking of the night at the Giving Tree launch when he and Shauna chatted over the Christmas Conversation Starters and he shared that same story with her. That was the night she grabbed his heart and wouldn't let go.

He and his mom didn't always agree on everything, but she was right in this instance. Selling her the inn would give him the freedom to pursue his own interests. His mom always said, *if you love what you do, you'll never work a day in your life.* That's exactly the kind of life he could have with an Outdoor Adventure touring company. Everything he had learned about the hospitality industry, he learned from Robin. If he succeeded in his new venture, he knew she would be well-pleased. She would not want his dreams, his life, to die with hers.

This new all-inclusive adventure would allow his guests to escape to the mountains, unplug, and connect to nature. Shauna had talked about starting her own agency. If he and Shauna had a future together, there was a chance he could convince her to stay in Spring Valley.

As soon as he had a strong cell coverage, he pulled over and tried calling Shauna. It went straight to voice mail. He was getting concerned. He decided he would stop at the cottage and tell her in person. He rang the bell. No answer. Knocked on the door. No answer. When he retreated to the SUV, he texted. No reply. Now he was very concerned.

He knew Big Papi needed a potty break and hoped he hadn't taken care of business on the kitchen floor. Gabe decided to go to the inn and take Big Papi for a walk on the path that led to Ryan's workshop. Maybe he knew something about Shauna.

He opened the woodshop's door and entered. He expected to hear the whining sounds of saws and sanders and see dust particles dancing in the air. Instead there were no machines running. There were no people working.

"Anybody here?" Gabe yelled.

A familiar voice answered. "Back here. Come through the middle door."

He and Big Papi walked through the door and found Ryan sitting astride on, what Gabe would describe as, a wooden horse. His feet were pressed on a treadle bar at the head of the wooden horse. A foot-activated clamp held the wood piece securely. With a drawknife in hand, he pulled over the greenwood, shaving a square piece into a round profile. Long ribbon shavings piled curled around his boots.

"I walked in and thought maybe everyone was out on an early lunch break." He motioned for Big Papi to sit. He sat with his tongue hanging out, and seemed to be as interested in the contraption as Gabe.

"No, the guys are off today. They chose to work ten-hour days, four days a week. I use that day for my old-timey mountain craft day." He smiled. "I bet you thought I was back here playing on a rocking horse." He grinned. "If you were, it's close. It's called a shaving horse and I do enjoy working on it."

"You know that I've been here several times, but I didn't realize you had a secret workshop."

"This is my old-timey sanctuary. My time to get back to my mountain roots." He pointed to a worn wooden tool chest. "Those are my papaw's tools. He was a chairmaker. The first woodworker in our family. They were simple folk-art chairs he sold that helped put food on the table. I make a few, now and then, just to keep the tradition." He pointed to the doorway. "There're no power tools allowed beyond that door. This is where everything is unplugged."

"Your talent is incredible."

"There's one thing I like the most about my old-timey days. My hands hold the same tools my dad and my papaw held." He cradled the tool. "I feel their presence."

Gabe envied the connection this family had with generations from the past.

"That's enough of me being an old sentimental fool. What's brings you around? Is there a problem with the fireplace mantle?"

"No. I think there may be a problem with your daughter."

"What's wrong with Shauna?"

"That's it. I don't know. I was hoping you could tell me." Gabe looked worried and sounded confused. "She was stressed last night from being out in nasty weather, so I dropped her off, and Santa and I delivered the rest of the packages. She asked me to text when I arrived back at the inn. I did and she didn't reply."

"I saw the lights in the drive last night when you dropped her off and called and we talked a few minutes." He shook his head in concern. "After we ended the conversation, I admit I was a little worried that she might have overdone it. I thought she was just tired." Trying to reassure Gabe, he said, "She probably just fell asleep and didn't respond to your text."

Gabe pulled up a work bench next to the shaving horse. He told Ryan about the morning calls, knocks on the door, and texts without response. He felt comfortable enough and compelled to share with Ryan his news, his worries, his dreams, his planned future with his daughter. They sat and talked like father and son. Ryan was fathering the fatherless.

Ryan knew his prayers had been answered. God brought Gabe and Shauna together. Shauna just needed to realize it.

Still using shaving horse as his chair, Ryan advised Gabe to give her time.

"I don't want Shauna to know what I'm about to tell you. I don't like keeping secrets, but you have to promise you won't tell."

Gabe raised his hand to swear an oath. "I won't say a word."

"Shauna said she shared her story with you,

how she was sexually harassed, then stalked. As you can imagine, it's been a difficult situation. She's strong, but from everything I've researched, just when you think you've tackled PTSD, it rears its ugly head and strikes."

Gabe didn't know if his heart could take the rest of the conversation. It beat hard in his chest.

"I haven't told Shauna, and I never will, that I set up a video conferencing appointment with her therapist, not for her to reveal any patient-client confidential information, but to advise me and Colleen on how to support her when she returned home for the holidays."

Gabe could read the concern in Ryan's face as he shared. "Shauna has been setting boundaries for so long. She had to. It was part of surviving and recovering. But, I think she's unintentionally built an emotional fortress to keep you out, because she's afraid to trust."

Gabe was bewildered. He thought she had allowed him in. He thought they had a future together. Ryan noticed that Gabe ran his hands through his hair and rubbed his neck, just as he did the night in the emergency waiting room. He wanted to give him hope of a future together with his daughter, but that future was ultimately up to Shauna.

"The roads were getting nasty last night. She may have had flashbacks to the accident. Post-traumatic stress can throw you into a tail spin. I don't know. But I do know that you've fallen head

over heels in love with my daughter, and I'm okay
with that. But, heed my words. I just think you
need to be patient and give her time."

That was the third time he'd advised Gabe
to give his daughter time.

Gabe's phone alerted him to a text message.
"Maybe this is her. Excuse me, let me check." He
pulled his phone out of his jacket pocket.

It read: *I'm okay. I don't want to disappoint
you, but I need some time to work through some
issues. I'll see you at the Giving Tree celebration at the
Mockingbird.*

Crestfallen, Gabe handed the phone to Ryan
to read.

He nodded his head and looked at Gabe.
"Don't give up. She's worth fighting for." He gave
him a backslap.

Gabe stood and Big Papi followed his lead.

Gabe understood why Shauna idolized her
father. He'd heard his words. He'd found wisdom.
He'd found a mentor.

#

Big Papi had a confusing walk home. He normally
could read his owner's moods. After they left the
building there was no sniffing, investigating, or
nose-rubbing allowed. First, he walked slow, ig-
noring his furry companion. He picked up his pace
about halfway home. Then, with the inn in sight,
he walked full speed ahead. Big Papi just mirrored
his friend's stride and as soon as they entered the
kitchen, he went for the water bowl. His friend

went who knows where.

#

On his walk home, Gabe only thought of one thing. Shauna. Gabe knew love. He also knew the pain of losing his love. Shauna was unexpected. He had no warning, she just walked into his life. No, he corrected himself, she dropped into his life like a tornado. Turned his heart upside down. He wrestled with his thoughts. Should he be cautious? He knew life could be taken away in a moment and vowed not to waste any precious time. Should he step away and give her the time she asked for? Or should he step out in faith and see where the path led. Maybe, he would do both.

Chapter Twenty-Six

By the time her one-woman rescue team arrived, Shauna had decided she would live the rest of her life cooped up in the cottage with chickens as her only friends. She shared her plan as Abby pulled the Chinese food out of the bag.

"I have my long-range plan for my future. It's simple. I'm hiding out right here in this cottage. My only chats will be conducted with chickens." Abby gave her a side glance, thinking she needed to check the pill bottle. "I will purchase t-shirts, in an assortment of colors, with my new identity in decorative print.' She used her index finger and thumb of both of her hands to form a frame. "CRAZY CHICKEN LADY and a silhouette of a chicken, just in case you had trouble reading the font choice."

Abby twirled her finger to her temple. "Crazy must run in our family. You've always called Mom, the Crazy Christmas Lady, now I guess it's your turn." She winked. "I'm just glad crazy skipped over me."

Shauna reached in the cabinet for drinking glasses, deciding on which to choose, she asked, "I can offer you the two W's. Wine or water?"

Abby preferred wine, but from the dark circles under Shauna's eyes, she thought it best to go with the other W. "Let's both have water."

Abby tossed her coat on the rack and went for the chopsticks. "I'm starving. Let's eat and talk. I picked up your favorite vegetable lo mein dish. I ordered the sweet and sour chicken. There's plenty if you want to share."

Shauna wasn't interested in eating, but she dished out a small portion of the lo mein and chose an eggroll. "I'm good with this. Thanks for dinner and the sleepover. But be warned, it will probably be more of a talk-over."

Abby wanted to dine before she discovered what had Shauna so upset. She always thought better after dining. She didn't know if she should be relieved Shauna was cracking chicken jokes, or worried she was drugged out of her mind.

"Is our soap opera recorded on your playlist? Let's watch, while we eat." She plopped on the couch, chopsticks in hand.

"Great, their drama trumps my drama. I see where I rate in this family."

"Come on. Live a little. It will be like old times. You and me at Gran's, watching her 'stories.' I won't even make you cover your eyes in the bedroom scenes."

Just as she lifted chopsticks to her mouth,

Shauna playfully whacked Abby with the throw pillow. Her sweet and sour chicken flew across the room. In a blink of an eye, the lazy cat leaped from the couch, pounced on its prey, batted it around a few swats, and then gobbled it down, leaving a trail of red sauce behind. She licked her lips, then looked over her shoulder for another helping. The sisters laughed so hard they almost fell off the couch.

After they got control of their giggles, in a click they became immersed in the lives, loves, and battles in Genoa City. For those few minutes they were reliving a childhood memory, sitting together on Gran's couch, when they didn't have a worry in the world.

"I never imagined growing up that my life would end up having as much drama as any soap opera." Shauna let out a big puff, followed by tears rolling down her cheeks.

Abby knew the serious talk had commenced.

Shauna told her the haunting nightmare of the man and beast stalkers, reliving the trauma of the accident, and the absence of Gabe in the dream. Abby listened. Her deep eyes revealed empathy.

"I thought I had chased away those dreams. It just hit me without warning. What could I have done differently?"

Abby was always free with telling people what they should or shouldn't do. "I'll tell you what you could have done differently. For one, try quitting tackling the world like a bull in a china shop. Two, how about not getting in a vehicle to deliver Christmas gifts on slick roads." She shook her head in disbelief. "For goodness sake, you are recovering from a car accident, what were you thinking?" She realized she was almost shouting and regretted her tone.

Shauna was hurt and frustrated. "I was thinking about granting Christmas wishes for underprivileged kids and struggling single moms – that's what I was thinking." Adrenaline took over. "I was also thinking I might have received more sympathy and support from my big sis. Evidently, I was wrong about that, too." The floodgate opened. Tears gushed.

Abby put her arm around her baby sis. Shauna rested her head on her shoulder. The clamor of shouting that rose in the banter quieted to more civilized tones.

"I'm sorry," said Abby.

Shauna knew there was a "but" coming, there was always a "but" with Abby.

"But, you do understand we are both right, don't you?"

Shauna knew she was right. She listened.

"Honey, this is real trauma you're dealing with. You slayed a giant. But that battle wreaked havoc on you. You're doing so well, but it's natural that you'll have setbacks. The accident re-traumatized you. You have to remember what you learned from your therapist. You've come so far with your coping skills, you're managing your stress, you've reconnected with us. I'm here for you, but maybe you need professional help to get you through this. Have you considered finding a therapist locally?"

"I don't want to start over with a new therapist."

"Have you checked to see if your therapist offers online therapy or virtual house calls?" She already knew the answer, but her mom had sworn her to secrecy.

"Now that you bring that up, I vaguely remember her saying she was launching that service. When I was in Atlanta, I didn't even consider video conferencing, I needed face-to-face therapy. But that's a good idea."

"You know, Shauna, you're in a unique position right now. You can build the life you want to live." Shauna gave her that cocked puppy-dog confused look. "Think about it. With your settlement you have the finances to do whatever you want. You're the best in your business, you could open your own agency."

"I've been thinking seriously about that lately. In my industry, all I need is broadband, a computer, and a phone. "

She needed her family, too. That's exactly what Abby had been praying for. She wanted her to come home to Spring Valley.

"You could start your business here. Since

you left for Atlanta, the Recovery Act made fiber broadband internet access available in the whole county. So, if you don't want to live next door to Mom and Daddy, you could live on top of a mountain, if you wanted." Abby had a plan in mind. "Then if you decide you want to relocate, you'll be stronger and you can go wherever you want. But, know this, I want you here." She squeezed her a little tighter.

"It's been good to be home. I almost talked myself out of coming. I'm glad I didn't."

"What happened to you, I wouldn't wish on my worst enemy. But it happened. It's part of your life's story, now. But with every passing day, you'll be stronger, you'll bounce back quicker with the next blow, and you'll get up and live another full day."

"You're starting to sound like Ada when she's in her preaching mode."

"Amen, sister. Is it working?"

"Maybe, a little."

"Will this new life you're building include Gabe?" Abby circled back around to what she thought was the real reason for Shauna's stress and confusion. "If you think there's a future with Gabe, you need to be open and honest with him about your past and how it affects you now."

"That's just it." Shauna lifted her head from Abby's shoulder, and turned to face her. "I don't think he's going to be part of my future. He left this cryptic voice mail saying he had a buyer for the inn and we needed to talk. I'm afraid he's going to pack up and leave."

"That doesn't sound right. I think you're reading between the lines." On the way to pick up the Chinese take-out order, Abby had a call from her mother who filled her in on Gabe's visit to Ryan's workshop. She was certain Shauna was jumping to the wrong conclusion.

"Maybe it was just a holiday fling for him and I'm stupid." She let out a big puff. "It's just like in Atlanta when I was dumped because my ex-boyfriend didn't want any part of my messy life."

Abby had to put a stop to this negative thinking and blabbed the whole story. She knew it wasn't her story to tell, but she told it anyway. She hoped it would shock Shauna into reality. She revealed the whole plan. Gabe's mom buying the inn, Gabe staying in Spring Valley, building a cabin and staring an outdoor adventure touring company. Visiting their dad and pouring his heart out, seeking advice and hoping he had a future with his daughter.

Shauna sat spellbound; she stared at Abby in disbelief. "So, what I'm hearing you say is – Gabe loves me?"

"It appears so. But the real question here is, do you love him?" Abby never minced words.

"I thought I did. Then after last night, I talked myself out of it because I thought he didn't feel the same. Now, I don't know what to think." The longer she babbled the tighter she twisted a long strand of hair that had fallen loose on her face. "Out of the blue, he just entered my life and brought hope with him. He's patient, he's kind, he's compassionate, he's gentle, he listens, he has this spiritual connection with God and the mountains, and" – she raised her hand to her heart – "his eyes melt my heart and touch my soul."

"I don't want to get all churchy on you, but you just listed the attributes of love in the scripture." Abby shrugged her shoulders. "Just sayin'."

Abby shook her head in exasperation. She stood and took Shauna's coat off the rack and tossed it her way. "Get up and put your coat on," Abby instructed.

"Where are we going? I thought we were having a sister slumber party?"

"I'm driving you and dropping you off at Gabe's. The two of you need to talk. Now!"

Chapter Twenty-Seven

It was half past eight when Gabe sat at the kitchen counter, jotting down plans for his new venture. It was perfect timing for the sale. The inn was renovated, ready for new owners, and a grand re-opening. All he had to do was sign the papers to make it official. Curiously, he wondered how many times the deed had been transferred from one person to another. How many signatures filled the guest registers since circa 1790? If the walls could talk they would tell stories of people. Stories of dignitaries and nobodies. Stories of love and stories of loss. A history of restoration. A legacy of hospitality. His story would be part of the legacy. In both mind and heart, he was beginning to fully understand this connection to the past and the legacy one leaves.

First, he would contact the real estate agent to purchase the parcel of land on the mountaintop. Then, he would hire a contractor to pop up a tiny house cabin for temporary lodging during the main cabin construction.

He lifted his coffee, took a sip. Big Papi barked, alerting him to a visitor. He jerked and his coffee dribbled down his shirt. He grabbed a dish towel to dab the mess and glanced toward the door. It was dark. The bulb had burned out on the motion light, he was unable to see who knocked on the door. He didn't anticipate he needed an attack dog, so he led him by the collar to the front room and closed the kitchen door.

When he opened the door, his prayer was answered.

Shauna stood at his doorway.

She was unexpected. He stood bewildered and stared at her. She stood shivering in the cold waiting for him to let her in.

"I'm not a figment of your imagination." She waved her hands in front of his face. "Abby dropped me off. It's cold out here. Can I come in?"

He smiled that smile that made her heart flip.

She looked up at him with pleading eyes.

"I'm sorry. Yes, come in. I just wasn't expecting you." Her comedic timing was perfect. He opened the door wide and stepped aside to let her in and quickly shut out the cold. He wanted to wrap his arms around her, kiss her, hold her, and never let her go. Instead, he chose the safe hospitable gentlemanly gesture and asked to take her coat. He helped slide it off and hung it on the antique brass coat hook mounted beside the entry. Before she could speak, he asked, "Can I get you coffee or cocoa?"

"No, I'm fine. I don't know how long I'll be

staying." She began to twist her hair. "I think I owe you an apology."

He walked toward her, touched her arm, and gestured toward the settee in the dining nook near the fireplace. She sat and tucked up her legs. Gabe took a seat next to her, rested his arm comfortably on the back of the settee and turned slightly to face her. "You don't owe me an apology."

"Yes, I do. I pushed you away today because of my false assumptions. I was projecting my fears of rejection onto you. "

"You don't have to explain anything to me."

"I want to explain. Abby set me straight tonight. Remember what I said about her, eating and gossiping are two of her favorite pastimes. I was bemoaning the thought of you selling your inn and packing up and leaving. I assumed I was just a holiday fling. Someone to be used and cast aside. Abby threw some reality in my face and told me the buyer was your mom, you were staying in Spring Valley, and starting an outdoor adventure touring company. Your concern for me and the visit you had with my dad, melted my heart."

He gave her a sly grin. "I wanted to be the one to share the big news, but I'll let Abby off the hook, it sounds like she's on my side."

"Believe me, she is. But I want you to understand why I reacted the way I did. I want you to understand me." The heat from the fire warmed her body, but she still trembled from nervousness.

"My life was traumatized and changed forever. I was happy. Advancing in my career. My future looked bright. Then life became chaotic and I lost my life as I knew it. I've worked so hard in recovery. I came home for the holidays because I needed to reconnect with my family. I knew I would never lose them or their love. Their love brought me home." Her eyes never wavered from his. "Then you happened. You gave me hope when I was hopeless. Love when I felt unlovely. You calmed my storm. Then I heartlessly shut you out."

She paused for a moment and looked down at her hands, which she held clasped together on her lap. She took a deep breath and looked back up to his eyes. "I'm here to tell you, I've fallen deeply in love with you. I'm also here to tell you that I'm a terrible mess and I have PTSD from my trauma. You're the first person to hear those words cross my lips." He reached over and held her hand. "I'm better, but I'm still on the long road to recovery. I'll have times when something triggers flashbacks and I'll be a mess for a while. I understand if that's something you can't deal with. I wouldn't think less of you if you walked away."

He pulled her close and kissed her lips gently. He softly put his forehead against hers and lingered as their heart and soul became as one. He brushed his lips on her brow and held her at arm's length to look at her eye to eye.

"My plan was to talk to you after the Giving Tree celebration tomorrow night. You said you needed time, but I don't know how much time we have. I've loved and I know the pain of losing love. When you were unconscious at the scene of the accident, I was afraid I would lose you forever. I'm stepping out in faith. Hoping you will at least hear me out." He lifted her hands to his lips and kissed them softly. "I don't care that your life is a mess. We all have messy lives. I don't want to spend Christmas without you." He kissed her hands again. "Life happened quickly. You happened. I've lived more in the last three weeks than I have in the last three years. These events that disrupted my life were unexpected. The fire, meeting you, the Giving Tree, the ornaments of hope wishes, the accident, the kids, selling the inn. It's been beyond all reason, yet each incident has been life altering."

He paused for a moment and caressed her face. "You've changed my life. I'm in love with you, Shauna Murphy. I know I couldn't have navigated this on my own, there's a higher plan, God has given me a higher calling. He gave me you. You're my divine Christmas gift. All of this has given me a greater meaning and purpose in my life. It forced me to see life in a whole new perspective. I'm no longer consumed with myself; I see beyond. I see people that truly need help." He paused again when little Gabriel's image drifted in his mind. His eyes stung. "It's made life come into focus. I'm starting to see how I fit in God's plan, how *we* fit in His plan. I think all of this has been a catalyst for me to see the life I want to live. The life I want to live – with you."

She threw her arms around his neck and their lips met in a warm loving kiss. As their lips parted she whispered, "Tell me again."

He framed her face in his hands. "Which part? I love you, you're my divine Christmas gift, or I don't ever want to spend a Christmas without you?"

"All the above!" She ran her fingers through his hair and brought his lips back to hers.

He would keep telling her not just for this Christmas, but for next Christmas. Forever. For all the Christmases the rest of their lives.

Chapter Twenty-Eight

Never in her wildest dreams did Ada ever imagine the miraculous results and generational impact of the Giving Tree campaign. Seeing through tears, she looked out over the standing-room-only crowd and shook her head, almost scolding herself. She shouldn't be surprised, she knew His words, God could do anything, far more than she could ever imagine or request. Through her Facebook account, she invited all those who participated to a celebration at her little sanctuary, which she disguised as the Mockingbird Coffee House, and they came – they came in droves. It didn't matter what their race, color, creed, or religion; they rolled up their sleeves and in the doctrine of "love conquers hate" they worked together to grant Christmas wishes to the needy of Spring Valley. She thanked the wishers, the facilitators, the donors, volunteers, and community partners that gave of themselves, their time, and finances to give the down-and-out in their community a dose of hope for Christmas. She chuckled, thinking to herself she had never seen so many people, so happy to depart with so much of their hard-earned money.

In the afternoon before the Giving Tree Celebration event began, Ada took an ornament off the tree and slipped it in her apron pocket for safe keeping. Pinching pennies, she had planned on saving all the trimmings for next year's tree, but she made an exception for this special circumstance. At the close of the evening, Ada handed Shauna a heart-shaped ornament. It was the ornament Shauna had selected three weeks earlier. It didn't surprise Ada that out of all the dozens of decorations on the tree, even with Shauna using her hand as a blindfold, she'd chosen the only heart-shaped ornament hanging on the tree. Ada commemorated it as their *keepsake ornament of hope*. A forever reminder of Shauna and Gabe's divine appointment and their story of love. She hugged Shauna and whispered in her ear, "The three greatest things are faith, hope, and love. But the greatest of these is love. I'm blessed you found love at the Mockingbird."

Ada waved at the Christmas couple and decided, the way she saw it, she and the Lord made a good matchmaking team. She whispered a prayer, "Thank you, Lord. They are truly a match made in heaven. Bless their lives."

Gabe and Shauna waved goodnight to Ada. They left holding hands with fingers tightly woven together and hearts full of love, hope, and dreams for their future. In their loss, they had discovered love.

#

Ada Taylor launched her army of volunteers of

hope on Sunday, November twenty-ninth at the Mockingbird Coffee House. Eighteen days later, every wish from the Giving Tree had been given. It inspired a movement of generosity in Spring Valley. It became one of the town's most treasured traditions, forever changing the way they celebrate Christmas, reminding us of the hope, love, and joy to be found in giving.

THE END

A Note from Georgia

A big heartfelt thank you for reading *The Ornament of Hope*! I hope you enjoyed Shauna and Gabe's story and found it to be an inspiration during this Christmas season. I pray for God's special Christmas blessing on you and yours.

If you did enjoy *The Ornament of Hope*, I would love for you to write a review. Reviews are a huge help to authors and I would love to read your feedback, and it's a great help for readers interested in one of my books for the first time.

You can post a review on Amazon or go to my website and leave a review message, sign up for New Releases in 2021, Encouraging Blog Posts, and Giveaways:
www.georgiacurtisling.com

Thank you and Christmas blessings!!

Georgia

About the Author

Born and raised in the foothills of the Appalachian Mountains, Georgia holds dear the three inherent mountain values of faith, family, and the land. Her debut Christmas romance novel, *The Ornament of Hope* is rich with voices from the past, memories of heartwarming stories, and traditions of her cherished heritage. She and her husband, Phil, live in Tennessee near their adult son, Philip and daughter-in-heart, Lauren.

Georgia Curtis Ling is the bestselling author of *What's in the Bible for Women.* She touches the heart and tickles the funny bone as she writes about faith, love and life. Over her career her work has appeared in numerous periodicals, and nine best-selling books, including the *God's Vitamin "C" for the Spirit series, God's Abundance,* and *God's Unexpected Blessings.*

New releases coming in 2021: *In Mom They Trust,* and *Moms Lead in Love* from the Moms in Faith Bible Study series, and the new eleven book Bible Study series you've been waiting for, *Bible Truths for Women: God's Advice for Being Your Best in Every*

Area of Your Life.
For release dates go to:
www.georgiacurtisling.com

Made in the USA
Coppell, TX
01 December 2020